"I want to kiss you."

Joel's voice was matter-of-fact. "Last time I didn't ask you. This time I am."

"Oh." Damaris swallowed, her eyes still fixed well below his chin. "I—I don't think that's a good idea."

"I don't see why not. I rather enjoyed it the first time. So did you."

"I—um—yes, I did." There was no point in denying it. "But as we won't be seeing each other again, it would seem—hypocritical."

"Oh, would it? And what makes you think we won't be seeing each other again?"

"But you only owed me one date!"

"So I've paid my debt. Now I'd like to take you out because I choose to. Not because I have to."

"Oh." Damaris's hand flew to the topaz necklace, twisting it. "I'm flattered. But I *don't* choose to."

Kay Gregory grew up in England, but moved to Canada as a teenager. She now lives in Vancouver with her husband, two sons, one dog and two ferrets. She has had innumerable jobs, some interesting, some extremely boring, which have often provided background for her books. Now that she is writing Harlequin romance novels, Kay thinks she has at last found a job that she won't find necessary to change.

Books by Kay Gregory

HARLEQUIN ROMANCE
2919—A STAR FOR A RING
3016—A PERFECT BEAST
3058—IMPULSIVE BUTTERFLY
3082—AMBER AND AMETHYST
3152—YESTERDAY'S WEDDING
3206—BREAKING THE ICE

HARLEQUIN PRESENTS
1352—THE MUSIC OF LOVE

Don't miss any of our special offers. Write to us at the following address for information on our newest releases.

Harlequin Reader Service
P.O. Box 1397, Buffalo, NY 14240
Canadian address: P.O. Box 603,
Fort Erie, Ont. L2A 5X3

AFTER
THE ROSES
Kay Gregory

Harlequin Books

TORONTO • NEW YORK • LONDON
AMSTERDAM • PARIS • SYDNEY • HAMBURG
STOCKHOLM • ATHENS • TOKYO • MILAN
MADRID • WARSAW • BUDAPEST • AUCKLAND

TO: EVERYONE AT YELLOWPOINT
With thanks for all the helpful suggestions.
TO: BETH & ADRIAN
Who conquered Grouse Mountain for me.
AND TO: DIANA
Who owns Candy the Cat.

Original hardcover edition published in 1991
by Mills & Boon Limited

ISBN 0-373-03243-9

Harlequin Romance first edition January 1993

AFTER THE ROSES

CHAPTER ONE

'GOOD grief!' exclaimed Damaris. 'What in the world is *that*?'

'What is *what*?' asked her companion, in a plummy voice. Mary Carmichael did not appreciate being interrupted in the middle of an indignant dissertation on the iniquities of a committee which had failed to elect her as president.

Damaris gestured across the ballroom at the object of her startled attention. 'That—that hunk of masked cardboard beefcake on the dais,' she stuttered, her eyes riveted on a life-sized cut-out of an impressively built man in an impressively expensive suit, whose possibly impressive features were concealed behind a fitted black mask which covered his face from eyebrows to just above a pair of inviting lips. Lips which looked familiar somehow—but Damaris didn't think she'd ever met their owner. . .

'Oh.' Mary shrugged her elegant shoulders, and her eyes slid evasively sideways. 'That's our mystery guest. Come along now—I believe this is our table.'

The table in question was a small one set just for two, with an excellent view of the dais which had been erected at the back of the room. Damaris noted that most of the other tables in this elite hotel ballroom, which doubled as a banquet facility, were set to accommodate six or eight people. She smiled to herself, thinking that as usual Mary had managed to be exclusive.

She waited until the black-gowned hostess had left

them before pursuing the intriguing matter of the unusual masked decoration.

'What mystery guest?' she asked.

Mary, who was toying with a napkin and looking uncharacteristically vague, cleared her throat and said quickly. 'After the dinner we're going to hold a raffle. The prize is an evening out with our—our guest.'

'What?' Damaris laughed disbelievingly. 'But who on earth would be crazy enough to buy a ticket for an evening with a man they've never met? He could be awful.'

Mary laughed too, a little over-brightly. 'Yes, I suppose he could, but after all the idea *is* to raise money for children whose parents aren't able to afford travel expenses for special medical treatments. We wouldn't pick an undesirable person, would we? That sort of mistake could do nothing but hurt the charity.'

'Mm. That's true, I suppose.' Damaris studied this friend, who was also her next-door neighbour, with deep scepticism. 'Mary, you've been trying to persuade me to start dating again for months. You don't imagine I'm buying a ticket on that man, do you? Because I'm not. Scott's been dead for a year and a half now, and I've no intention of getting involved again.'

'Hm! You're too young to be alone, Damaris. You need a man to help you raise your daughter.'

'I'm twenty-seven, I'm raising my daughter perfectly well on my own, thank you, and I am *not* buying a ticket for that chunk of masked cardboard over there.'

Mary raised a delicate eyebrow. 'I believe he also has flesh, my dear. Quite nice flesh.'

'Yes,' agreed Damaris, glancing across the room at the powerfully built figure with the large hands, strong neck and aggressively square cleft chin. 'I expect he has. But I'm not buying him.'

'Well, it's hardly a question of—no, of course you aren't, dear.' Mary capitulated with what, for her, was unusual passivity.

'Why don't *you* try to win him?' suggested Damaris.

The other woman shook her head. 'I'm too old for that sort of thing.'

Damaris stifled a chuckle. In her early forties, Mary, reputed to have been the Honourable Mary before her brief marriage to a Canadian banker had uprooted her from a family estate in Yorkshire, was by no means too old for 'that sort of thing'. She was just too busy organising everyone else's lives to have any interest in acquiring anything or anyone who might want to curb her aggressively charitable activities. Even so, it was generally assumed she meant well.

The ballroom was filling rapidly now, and as Damaris began to take in her surroundings she was puzzled to observe that all the guests seemed to be women. Her friend had apparently forgotten to mention *that* little detail too. Not that it made much difference.

When Mary had first brought up the matter of this charity dinner, she had informed Damaris, with her standard disregard for anyone else's wishes, that she had bought her a ticket. Which meant that, as far as Mary was concerned, her young neighbour's attendance was now a foregone conclusion. But Damaris, who often fell in with Mary's plans because it saved a lot of trouble and ill-feeling, had drawn the line at that.

'I'll come,' she had said, 'but I'm buying my own ticket. I can afford it. And it's certainly a worthy cause.'

She knew that if she let Mary buy the ticket her bossy neighbour would feel that Damaris owed her a favour.

Probably several favours. After which her life wouldn't be her own.

Mary had given in with surprising mildness. 'Just as long as you accompany me,' she had agreed, nodding graciously.

Now, amid the busy hum of female conversation, the black-garbed waiters began to serve bouillabaisse and wine.

By the end of an excellent meal, Damaris was beginning to feel relaxed and mellow. She murmured soothingly agreeable platitudes in response to Mary's continued grumbles about the short-sighted committee which had not elected her, and, by twisting her chair a little to the right, she managed to avoid a direct view of the cardboard hunk across the room. She didn't know why, but she found that odd, inanimate presence strangely disturbing.

Then, when the last plates had been unobtrusively removed from the tables, there was a sudden lull in the animated feminine chatter. The three-man band seated beneath the cut-out on the dais began to play a soft, romantic tune. On the other side of the room someone gave a nervous giggle. As the tempo of the music increased, the lights of the ballroom were dimmed—and in the glare of a single spotlight the flesh and blood manifestation of the mystery man strode out from behind a curtain. He was wearing evening dress and his mask, and his curving mouth tightened for a moment as he took his place beside a tall, toothy woman with a lot of blonde hair piled up on top of her head.

Wow, thought Damaris, in spite of herself. Flesh and blood indeed. *And* he knows it.

The figure on the dais wasn't exceptionally tall, but he had a presence. The sort of presence it would have been impossible to ignore, even without the concentration of the spotlight. He held himself rigidly erect, with his shoulders back and his cleft chin jutting assertively. He looked commanding, arrogant, and the sensuous lips she had noted earlier were pulled into a twisted curl that seemed designed to let the assembled company know that he was doing them an enormous favour, at the cost of considerable boredom—and probably inconvenience—to himself.

Arrogant bastard, thought Damaris. All the same, she couldn't take her eyes off him. And somewhere she *had* seen those lips before. They weren't the sort of lips one would forget. . .

'Well?' whispered Mary. 'What do you think?'

Damaris wasn't obliged to answer, because just then the woman with the toothy smile stepped in front of the microphone to announce breathlessly, 'And now, ladies, the moment we've all been waiting for. . .'

'I haven't,' muttered Damaris, as Mary shushed her.

'The moment when our mystery man will choose his fate—er, date.' She tittered, and flashed her teeth so broadly that Damaris expected them to fall out. 'Sir. . .' the blonde turned coyly to the overpowering figure beside her '. . .will you pick your ticket now, please?' Incongruously she held out a slightly battered felt hat.

The mystery man turned towards her and somehow contrived to look as if he had barely moved. Then his hand was extracting a strip of white paper from the hat and snapping it open.

'Would you care to announce the name of the lucky winner?' gurgled the blonde.

The mystery man lifted his head, still managing to look as if he were above these plebeian proceedings—

which of course he was, literally, thought Damaris, trying not to giggle.

It was the last time she felt like giggling that evening, because a moment later the man was opening his mouth to announce in a deep, drawling voice that didn't sound delighted at all, 'I'm delighted to inform you that the — ah—lucky winner is Ms C Damaris Gordon of West Vancouver.'

There was a quick buzz of curiosity, disappointment— and perhaps in some cases, relief—as faces turned to peer across the room searching for the unknown Damaris Gordon—who was trying to sink invisibly into her chair as she gazed, horrified, at her companion, and managed to blurt out, 'Mary! It must be a mistake. I didn't buy a ticket.'

'You didn't have to, dear,' replied Mary complacently. 'Your dinner ticket made you eligible for the draw.'

Damaris closed her eyes, wondering how many years she'd get for cracking a wine decanter over Mary's thick and very smug skull. When she opened them again, the mystery man was in the process of removing his mask— and in the next heart-stopping instant she knew why those lips had been familiar.

'Joel Agar,' she gasped. 'The man with the platinum touch. No wonder I thought I knew him. His picture's in the paper all the time.'

'Yes, dear, aren't you lucky?' Mary, who had obviously been privy to the secret, was visibly purring.

'Did you fix this?' hissed Damaris, her fingers still itching to pick up the decanter.

'Of course not. That is——'

'You didn't, because they wouldn't let you, but you tried to,' finished Damaris, her shoulders sagging.

'I suppose you could put it like that.'

She didn't want to put anything any way. She wanted to get up and run. But now the toothy woman was demanding that the holder of the winning ticket stand up—and, before Damaris could stop her, Mary, who was a large and healthy specimen of English womanhood, had grabbed her from behind and was hauling her on to her feet.

She took a deep breath. Mary had got her into this, and she would settle that score later. Meanwhile, she was not going to be manoeuvred into making an exhibition of herself in front of hundreds of people and, more than likely, the Press. All she could do was carry this appalling situation off with as much poise and grace as she could muster.

Which might not be much at all, she realised, panic-stricken. For now Joel Agar, British Columbia's best-known entreprenuer, owner of a dozen wildly successful car dealerships, and financial wheeler and dealer beyond compare, was descending from the dais and walking purposefully towards her. He was smiling, but it was a tight-lipped smile and there was no matching warmth in his eyes. Deep, amber-brown eyes with heavy lids, she saw as he came up to her. Bedroom eyes, that did horribly disconcerting things to her stomach. Which was ridiculous, because Joel Agar wasn't likely—luckily—to have any bedroom inclinations towards her. *She* might be looking at a man with wide cheekbones and a straight flared nose who, although not conventionally handsome, was none the less incredibly male. *He*, on the other hand, could only be seeing a skinny, round-faced young woman in a plain white dress, with ordinary grey eyes and short, mouse-coloured hair that formed a fluffy cap around her head. Not at all the type to attract the great tycoon. Not that he had been prepared to be attracted to anyone, she reflected, judging from his bored stance on the dais.

'Good evening, Ms Gordon. This is indeed a pleasure.' Joel Agar, a mystery no longer, was extending a condescending hand. And the stock phrase issuing from his lips sounded forced and patronising.

Damaris, holding herself rigidly upright in order to control an infuriating trembling in her limbs, extended an equally cool hand and said politely, 'Thank you. I'm sure the pleasure will be mine.'

It wouldn't, though, because she had no intention of going on a date with this man, whenever that date was meant to happen. It was a matter of getting through a disastrous evening without giving the other participants in this exhibition any cause for scandalised gossip.

She saw that, for the first time since he had entered the ballroom, Joel Agar was looking surprised instead of superior. And at once she realised why. It was her voice, of course. Deep, musical and alluringly at odds with her insignificant appearance, it always startled people at first. But they soon got over it when they came to the conclusion that their first impression of a quiet, rather ordinary young woman was correct.

Now that the formal and obligatory greetings had been exchanged, Damaris and her 'prize' stood sizing each other up. Warily. At least she supposed that that was wariness she saw in the amber-brown eyes. Then Joel Agar seemed to recollect himself. He was still holding her hand, and at once he dropped it as if her touch might contaminate him. With what particular plague she wasn't sure, but just for a second she wished he hadn't dropped it. And then wished she hadn't wished it.

'Well, Ms Gordon,' he said, making a visible effort to

behave as she supposed he thought prizes ought to behave, 'may I join you?'

Damaris groaned inwardly. Did this mean she was supposed to sit down with this man—and the perfidious Mary—while several hundred well-heeled women watched them avidly, hoping for vicarious romance?

It seemed there was nothing for it, and she was about to concede as graciously as possible when the band struck up a purposeful rendition of 'Oh, How We Danced on the Night We Were Wed', and the assembled company laughed delightedly and began to clap their hands.

Joel Agar raised his eyebrows. 'It seems we're expected to dance,' he remarked without enthusiasm. 'May I have the pleasure?'

Damaris, irked beyond endurance by his obvious boredom and reluctance, said acidly, 'If you insist. But if there's any pleasure involved, Mr Agar, in this case I'm afraid it will be all yours.'

She was pleased to note that that shook him. About time. Apparently Mr Platinum Fingers expected her to swoon into his arms just because he had wealth, position, influence and—yes, she had to admit it—a very powerful sexual aura.

But now, to her utter amazement, she saw that he was smiling, and this time the smile seemed genuine. It was also remarkably attractive.

'Well, I'm damned,' he murmured. 'The little white mouse has a sharp tongue to go along with that come-hither voice.'

'I'm not a mouse,' replied Damaris through nearly clenched teeth. 'And, quite frankly, I would greatly prefer it if *you* went thither.'

The smile turned into a broad grin, which produced a watery sensation in her knees.

'At the moment I'm much more interested in my own preferences,' he informed her, 'and, strangely enough, I prefer to dance with you. Besides, I believe it's expected of us. Come on.'

With startling briskness he snapped his fingers around her wrist and pulled her on to the small polished space in the centre of the room which had evidently been kept clear for just this purpose. Then his arm was clasped masterfully around her waist and he was holding her close, but not quite touching his body, as the band began to play again from the beginning. Feeling like a leaf borne along by a gale-force wind, Damaris had no option but to follow.

She was not a good dancer. She had never had much opportunity to learn. But in this man's arms she felt as light and sure-footed as a ballerina. The clapping in the background grew louder, and the band switched suddenly to an upbeat, fiery little tune with which she was not familiar.

Her partner took the opportunity to pull her closer, and now she was pressed against him, feeling the breadth and hardness of his chest even through the heavy fabric of his jacket. To her horror, she found she had to make a conscious effort not to let her arm creep up around his neck. It felt right somehow, safe, here in his embrace, circling the small dance-floor—with hundreds of people looking on. Then his hand slipped lower on her waist, and she thought she felt something else. She glanced up, startled, and saw that his lips were twisted in an amused, very explicit smile. And, contrary to her expectations, that bedroom look in his eyes was most definitely directed at her.

She swallowed nervously and tried to pull away, but

at that moment the music stopped and immediately he let her go and led her decorously back to the table.

Mary beamed up at them, and Damaris felt the urge to murder return.

'Thank you,' she said, turning to her partner and trying to look cool and unaffected.

She waited for him to say 'my pleasure' again, but he didn't because at that moment a waiter came bustling up to hand him a folded slip of paper.

He gave it a cursory glance, then bowed with a studied politeness which betrayed no hint of the invitation she could have sworn she had seen in his eyes.

'I'm afraid I have to leave you,' he said smoothly. 'Something's come up. A small emergency.'

Damaris made a determined effort to suppress a stab of disappointment—and succeeded. 'Of course,' she said, equally smoothly. 'It's been—delightful.'

There. Scott would have been proud of her. She'd managed to sound like Lady Bracknell and the Queen of Sheba combined. She extended a ladylike hand.

Joel Agar took it, and she saw that the edge of his mouth was turning up suspiciously.

'Delightful indeed. Until you claim your prize then, Ms Gordon. I'll look forward to it.'

'No, wait,' gulped Damaris. 'I mean, there's no reason for us to meet again——'

'Of course there is. You've paid for me, haven't you? And you're going to get me. I always make good my debts.'

Oh, dear. She didn't like the sound of that.

She was still trying to decide how to reply when he released her hand, nodded to Mary, said, 'Good evening,' with studied courtesy, and walked away. The last Damaris saw of him was his broad back disappearing through a distant door, as she noticed for the first time that his businesslike short brown hair had a tendency to curl rebelliously at the neck.

'Mary,' said Damaris, sinking heavily into her chair, 'I'm going to kill you.'

'I don't see why, dear. I've met Joel Agar several times. He's quite a nice man.'

'Quite nice men aren't conceited enough to think they're every woman's dream of the perfect date. And anyway, I don't need a man.'

'Yes, you do. And we *asked* him to be our mystery date. He did it just for the charity.'

'Not to mention his ego,' muttered Damaris. 'And I suppose that "emergency" was prearranged so he wouldn't have to invest too much of his precious time.'

'I don't know about that. I think he *was* expected to stay for a little longer.'

'Anyway, I'm not going out with him,' snapped Damaris. '*You* can have him.'

'I didn't have a ticket,' replied Mary. 'At least, I did—but I made sure it wasn't in the hat.'

'And that mine was.'

'Don't sulk, dear. It'll do you good to get out.' She leaned across the table and gave her irate young friend a patronising pat on the hand.

Damaris snatched it away. 'It's time we left,' she said, almost rudely. 'Mary, I know that you meant well, but please don't ever do that again.'

'Maybe I won't have to,' the target of her wrath replied archly.

Damaris gave up.

'Chloe, you don't really think he'll phone, do you?'

It was the following afternoon and Damaris, in need

of a confidante, had hurried across to visit her only next-door neighbour besides Mary in the quiet cul-de-sac to which Scott had brought her three years ago on their marriage. Now she was sharing a deep armchair with an assortment of pencils and six newspapers, and holding her sleeping daughter on her lap.

Chloe tossed her untidy dark hair behind her shoulder. 'Of course he will. I was talking to Mary this morning. She says the arrangement was for him to meet the lucky winner—in this case, you—at the dinner last night, and then to get in touch with you later to settle on a suitable evening——'

'Well, there won't *be* any suitable evenings. Chloe, did you know about this?'

'I did not. I get very tired of Mary's meddling, and as far as I'm concerned you're quite capable of arranging your life for yourself.' Chloe stared at a ball of fluff which had just blown on to the rug, and added reminiscently, 'She tried to marry me off once. Imagine that. Men are wonderful, but I sure wouldn't want to face the same one on my pillow every morning. Not that I'm likely to find one who'd be crazy enough to have me.'

Damaris laughed. There wasn't any tactful answer to that because Chloe, who probably made a great deal of money from the unusual brass jewellery she designed, lived and dressed like a thirty-year-old refugee from the sixties. And it was hard to imagine that any man *would* be interested in a permanent relationship with a very independent lady who couldn't cook anything that didn't smell like last week's dirty socks, and who, although she presumably had nice furniture under the casual piles of litter around her house, seemed never to have discovered a use for drawers or cupboards.

'What's he like?' asked Chloe now, throwing a long,

flowered skirt off a chair and plumping herself down across from Damaris.

'Oh, average height but he seems taller, well-built, nice dark brown hair that could be a little longer, strange, rather fascinating eyes—and lips. . .' Damaris's voice trailed off and her grey eyes grew transparently dreamy.

'Hmm,' grunted Chloe. 'And you're trying to make me believe you don't want to go out with him?' She twisted a wide brass bangle around her wrist. 'What's he *like* though, Damson? I know he's attractive: I've seen his picture often enough—usually after he's just closed some deal that's added another couple of million to his coffers.'

'He donates a lot of it though,' said Damaris. And then, wondering why she had felt the need to defend him, she added quickly, 'He's an arrogant brute. You should have seen him on that dais, looking terribly bored and disdainful and as though he was conferring a terrific honour on all us poor panting females. Imagine spending an evening with a man who behaves as if he's manna from heaven.'

Chloe grinned. 'Sounds a bit like our Mary. *She* thinks we're all a bunch of colonials who need civilising, grooming and generally shaping up.' She hesitated, and then asked doubtfully, 'How are you going to get out of it though, do you think?'

'I'll tell him I can't get a babysitter for Ginny.'

'That's a good one.' Chloe smiled. 'He'll never believe you. A woman who can afford a ticket to that dinner, but can't, in the entire Lower Mainland, find a sitter——'

'I'm particular about my sitters,' said Damaris, pulling

a face at her friend and smoothing her two-year-old daughter's flaxen head.

Chloe shrugged. 'Oh, well, it'll serve Mary right if you don't go. The charity will be embarrassed and say it's all her doing.'

Damaris looked down at Ginny and didn't answer. At the moment she wasn't much interested in Mary's feelings—assuming she had any beyond a pressing need to run everything and everyone her own way.

A few minutes later Ginny began to wake up, so Damaris left Chloe stirring something dubious on the stove and returned to her own tidy split-level next door.

It was a big house, much too large for the two of them really, but when Scott had bought it—without even consulting her—he had envisioned several children along with attendant nannies and servants. As it was, Damaris managed it on her own with the help of a cleaning service which came in once a week. She had never quite got over the feeling that live-in help was a sinful extravagance as well as an intrusion on her privacy—which she guarded as a priceless treasure because to her that was precisely what it was.

She had just tucked Ginny into her pink and white cot when the phone rang. It was across the hall in her own room and she tripped over the cat as she ran to answer it, so she was a little breathless by the time she lifted the receiver.

'Ms Gordon?' enquired a deep, drawling voice she would never forget.

'Yes, this is Damaris Gordon.' She knew her own voice was less controlled than usual, and she wished she hadn't hurried to the phone.

'Damaris—may I call you Damaris?'

'If you wish.'

'I wish. And you can call me Joel.'

'Magnanimous of you.'

'Isn't it? What a pity your manners haven't improved since our last meeting.'

'There's nothing wrong with my manners. But as we obviously have nothing to say to one another——'

'Oh, but we have. I'll be over to pick you up in an hour.'

'Mr Agar——'

'Joel.'

'Joel, I am *not* going out with you tonight.'

'Yes, you are. I've already made the arrangements.'

'But I told you there was no need to carry on with this ridiculous business——'

'I know you did. And I told you that as you'd bought me you were damn well going to get me.'

'But I don't *want* you.'

He paused for just a fraction of a second, and then said with infuriating composure, 'We'll see about that. Be ready in an hour.'

'I'm busy tonight,' snapped Damaris, beginning to lose her temper.

'No, you're not. I checked with the Honourable Mary.'

Damn Mary, thought Damaris, not for the first time. Did she *have* to know everyone's business?'

'I'm still busy,' she insisted.

'So am I, so let's stop wasting each other's time, shall we? You get ready, and I'll be over to collect you at. . .' he paused '. . .seven o'clock.'

'I won't be here.'

'I think you will.'

Before Damaris could come up with a suitably cutting response, he had hung up the phone.

CHAPTER TWO

'How dare he?' Damaris demanded of no one in particular, and with the receiver still clutched uselessly in her hand. 'Of all the incredible nerve. . .' Her eye fell on the large calico cat which had followed her into the bedroom, her bushy tail twitching. 'Sorry, Candy. I didn't see you.'

Candy's yellow eyes were flat and disapproving as she stalked across to the big rosewood bed beneath the window and settled herself comfortably on to the pillows.

Damaris glared at a set of silver brushes on the matching rosewood dressing-table. What on earth was she supposed to do now? She had less than an hour in which to make herself and her sleeping daughter scarce, or else to get herself ready for—goodness knows what.

She had totally forgotten her excuse about the babysitter the moment she had heard that deep male voice on the line. And in any case, as Chloe had pointed out, the excuse was nonsense. Both Jane Spencer and her younger sister, who lived just one block away, were always anxious to earn extra money looking after children. And Ginny adored them. No, that wasn't the problem. The problem, in a nutshell, was Joel Agar.

'How dare he?' she muttered again. What right had he to go calling Mary, of all people, to ask what she, Damaris, was doing? She had made it quite clear last night that she wasn't interested in seeing him again, and in spite of that he had calmly gone ahead and made arrangements—without even troubling to ask her. That was exactly the sort of thing Scott would have done, she reflected, and she could do without any more of it. She shook her head, still unable to believe his nerve. Imagine phoning her up to inform her, as if she had no choice in the matter, that she was to get herself ready to go out. . .

Hold it, Damaris. She pulled herself up short. The fact was, of course, that she *did* have a choice. She glanced at her dainty jewelled watch. Yes, and she had precisely forty minutes in which to make it.

'Come on, Damaris,' she exhorted the face in the mirror. 'There *isn't* any choice. You've got to wake up your peacefully sleeping child and high-tail it back to Chloe's.'

No. That might not be far enough, because that infuriatingly high-handed man was more than capable of pursuing her at least as far as next door. It was the obvious bolt-hole.

She bit her lip. What then? Where should she go?

'Go with him, of course,' replied a voice which seemed to come out of nowhere. Startled, she glanced at the cat, but Candy was purring quietly on the bed. Then she realised, with a stab of incredulous outrage, that the voice was her own, and that the words were forming in her own traitorous head.

She sat down abruptly beside Candy. Oh, no. This was insane. She'd had her fill of overbearing, egotistical men, and she had made a deliberate and conscious decision, after Scott, that there wouldn't be any more of them in her life. So why was she even *thinking* about Joel Agar who, from what she'd seen of him, overbore and out-egoed them all.

Because, said the voice, this time silently, you, who thought you were through with men, find him quite unbearably attractive. And you can't get those eyes out of your head. *Or* those impossibly inviting lips, or. . .

Hell! Damaris jumped up again, causing Candy to open a bleak yellow eye. Now what? Should she run like a rabbit and trust time to cure her of this aberration? Or should she take the bull by the horns, go out with him, inevitably become even more disenchanted with his conceit and arrogance, and thus cure herself of a delayed attack of unexpectedly raging hormones?

She sighed. It was no contest really. In her own quiet, determined way, she had been facing challenges for the better part of her life. And overcoming them. Mr Agar would be no exception.

Besides—she grinned at herself in the mirror, feeling suprisingly giddy and light-hearted now that the decision had been made—the truth was, as Chloe had known right away, she *wanted* to see him again.

Damaris's upbringing had taught her very early on that if one wished to avoid dire consequences it was unwise to waste much time getting dressed. As a result, twenty minutes later, wearing a pale gold dress that moulded her figure discreetly without over-emphasising its thinness, she was seated in her airy living-room waiting coolly for Jane Spencer to arrive.

The teenager showed up almost at once and, after listening to a list of instructions from her employer which she already knew by heart, disappeared into the television-room.

Damaris resumed her seat by the red brick fireplace and pretended to read a book about gardening.

At seven o'clock on the dot, as Damaris was going over the same paragraph for the sixth time in a row without seeing it, the doorbell rang with a loud, imperative peal. By the time she reached the door it had rung twice more.

'I'm sorry you had to wait, but I'm fresh out of wings,' she informed the imposing figure in the dark suit who stood on her doorstep with his hand raised ready to press the bell again.

The hand dropped abruptly. 'You're what?'

'Fresh out of wings. You see I normally *walk* to the door when someone calls.'

'Hm.' His eyes flicked over her quickly, took in the clinging pale gold dress, and appeared to find no fault with what he saw. Then he started again, from the bottom, his gaze raking insolently over her legs, boyishly slim hips and small, neat breasts, to return with leisurely appreciation to her face. 'Very charming, my dear. It's a pity I can't say the same about your tongue.'

Damaris glowered, the giddy optimism she had felt earlier evaporating as though it had never been.

'You can hardly expect me to welcome you with open arms,' she said frigidly. 'I did tell you I was busy tonight.'

'You did. But as it was a rather poorly disguised lie I had some reason to expect a courteous welcome. We'll get to the open arms later. Aren't you going to ask me in?'

Damaris stood aside with her small nose pointed well in the air, and didn't even deign to answer. If he thought she was going to open her arms to him later, he had another think coming. No doubt it would be a salutary shock.

Joel gave her a mocking smile as he walked past her, and took up a stand with his back to the mirror which hung above the big brick fireplace. 'You have excellent taste, Ms Damaris Gordon,' he observed, nodding at the comfortable white sofa and chairs, patterned mosaic tables and colourful bowls of flowers which brightened the room.

'Thank you. And it's Mrs Gordon.' Damaris walked casually across to the sofa and sat down.

'You don't say?' His eyebrows rose in what she took to be either criticism or derision. Then he rested an arm on the mantel and drawled softly, 'Your husband must be a remarkably accommodating man to let you buy tickets for strange men.'

'No, he's a remarkably dead man. And he wasn't accommodating in the least.'

'I'm sorry.'

His tone was so abrupt that Damaris decided not to ask whether he was sorry that Scott was dead or sorry that he hadn't been accommodating.

'It's all right,' she said briefly.

He nodded. 'Mm. Yes, perhaps it is. I'm not in the habit of appropriating other men's property. Other than on a strictly business basis.'

Why was it that he couldn't open his mouth without making her want to hit him? 'I wasn't Scott's property,' she snapped. 'I was his wife.'

Joel rubbed his hand over the back of his neck. 'Yes, of course you were. Tactless of me.'

'My goodness, do you mean you're actually admitting to a fault, Mr Agar? I didn't realise you had any.'

His eyes glinted. 'My name is Joel, as I believe I've already told you. And I have a great many faults. Until today one of them has not been violence against women.' He paused meaningfully. 'But I have a feeling that if I spend much more time in the vicinity of your waspish tongue, my dear, that inhibition might very well disappear.'

Damaris eyed him warily. He looked very male and

aggressive standing there lounging against the fireplace
with his normally neat hair beginning to fall enticingly
across his forehead. Quite capable of violence. He also
looked quite breathtakingly attractive. And she *had* been
baiting him inexcusably. On the other hand, she mused,
he'd asked for it. So now perhaps they were even.

She smiled suddenly, and the smile lit up her serious
little face, changing it completely and causing Joel to
pull in his breath.

'I wouldn't try anything, if I were you,' she said, her
low voice firm but no longer hostile. 'Even though you
have been provoked.'

'Provoked!' he exclaimed. 'I've been insulted, verbally
battered, infuriated, irritated—and told, in so many
words, that I'm an arrogant swine. I suppose you could
call that provocation.'

Damaris peered up at him doubtfully. He sounded
terribly irate, but—was that a hint of a smile she saw
tugging at one corner of his mouth? If it was, she didn't
think he wanted her to know it.

'You've done a fair bit of provoking yourself,' she
reminded him cautiously, not sure how he would take it.

To her surprise and relief, he grinned. 'So I have,' he
admitted. 'Shall we call a truce, then, and try to enjoy
the rest of our evening?'

Damaris grinned back. 'If you like. Provided you stop
telling me what to do. I'm not one of your employees,
you know.'

Joel raised his eyes to the ceiling. 'For which the Lord
has made me truly thankful,' he murmured, with unflat-
tering fervour. 'All right, Damaris, I'll try to stop telling
you what to do—if you'll make some effort to curb that
acid tongue.'

Damaris stifled a now familiar urge to kick him, and

stood up. 'It's a deal,' she conceded, extending a businesslike hand.

'Good.' He took it, and held on to it a shade too long. 'I know a very pleasant way of sealing deals,' he purred unexpectedly, his eyes transmitting an unmistakable message.

When her only response was a severely repressive glare, he heaved an exaggerated sigh and said, 'Never mind. We can see about that later too.'

A short time afterwards, following further unnecessary instructions to Jane, during which Joel stood in the living-room strumming his fingers on his thigh and looking as if Ginny were a thoroughly unwelcome surprise—as she probably was—they finally made their way down the path towards his car.

'Oh,' cried Damaris, just as they reached the gate. 'There's Candy. She isn't supposed to be outside after dark.'

'Candy?' repeated Joel, looking impatient. 'Who the hell is Candy? And it's not dark.'

'My cat. And it will be before we get back.'

'Good heavens. You mean you have a cat as well as a daughter?'

'Is there something wrong with cats?' she asked belligerently, bending down to pick up the errant feline.

'Probably not, if you happen to like them. I don't.'

'You wouldn't,' muttered Damaris under her breath.

Joel heard her and sent a very stern stare in her direction.

'OK, OK, I promised a truce,' she conceded. 'Just a minute while I put her back inside.'

There was a definite stiffness between them as Joel helped her into the car, which, she now realised with a start, was a very smart black Jaguar. The sort of car that attracted envious attention while giving an impression of quietly aggressive power.

'Don't you like children either?' she asked, after they had driven a short distance in total silence.

'Not particularly. I've encountered the odd one I can tolerate. Does that make me a monster?'

'No, not necessarily. What does a child have to do to be—tolerable—in your estimation?'

'Sit quietly in a corner and read a book?' he suggested, with a sideways smile she suspected was meant to annoy her.

'They don't come like that,' she responded, remembering the incessant squabbling and squealing that had gone on among the children she'd grown up with.

'I did,' said Joel.

'You would.'

'Aha. The return of the wasp. I didn't think you could do it.'

'Do what?'

'Be civil to me for more than five minutes.'

She looked away from him at the April sun dappling the road between the trees. It was true. She had enormous difficulty being polite to this man. It was very strange, because normally she avoided arguments unless arguing would serve some useful purpose. She took a deep breath.

'I'm sorry. I don't mean to be rude. But, you see, this is all a mistake. It was Mary's doing.'

'Mary?'

'Mary Carmichael. My neighbour.'

'Ah, yes. My source of information about your movements. I used to do business with her husband. Did you know there's a rumour on Howe Street that he staged his own death by drowning, and is now living peacefully in

South America—where his lady wife can't organise his life?' He stared blandly ahead at the road.

Damaris laughed. 'No, I hadn't heard that. But of course it's rubbish.'

'Of course. But tell me, what has the remarkable Mary got to do with your appalling manners?'

'My——' She stopped abruptly because the gleam in those extraordinary eyes was one of manifest incitement—to riot, probably—and she wasn't rioting in this beautiful car which was now running ever so smoothly up the Capilano Road.

'My manners are usually quite good,' she said, with a mildness that cost her some effort. 'At least they are when you're not around. No, wait,' she added quickly, as his head turned. 'What I'm trying to say is that I didn't even know I'd bought a ticket for you. If I *had* known, I wouldn't have done it.'

'Thank you.'

Damaris gave a sigh of exasperation. 'I don't mean that exactly. At least, I do, but. . .'

'Suppose you start at the beginning,' he suggested drily.

Damaris did, and, when she'd finished, to her amazement, Joel flung back his head and let out a roar of laughter.

'Well, I'll be damned,' he exclaimed, still chuckling. 'And to think I took you for some society airhead with a lot more money than brains.'

'I'm glad you concede that a lady with brains wouldn't buy you,' she murmured, nettled.

'My goodness,' groaned Joel. 'You just don't know when to stop, do you? I must have been out of my mind to insist that you collect your winnings.'

'Why did you?' asked Damaris curiously. 'You looked

thoroughly disgusted with the whole thing last night. As though you were above such triviality. Or are you determined to pay your debt because you find it hard to believe that there's a woman on earth who might not be panting to go out with you?'

'I think,' said Joel softly, pulling the car abruptly to the side of the road, 'that my personal prohibition on violence against women has just ended.' He switched off the engine, stretched his arm along the back of the seat, and turned to face her.

Damaris gulped. There were no houses on this stretch of road, and the tall firs towering above them cast long shadows in the evening sun.

'What do you mean?' she asked warily, uncomfortably conscious of the square-tipped fingers resting loosely next to her ear.

'I mean that I've had about all I'm going to take from you for the moment. We have met precisely twice, I have done my best to be nice to you—which isn't easy—and I've kept my part of the bargain, although I realise now it was a bargain you didn't know you'd made. In return I've had insults and abuse heaped upon my head by a woman with the face of a baby angel—and the tongue of a militant wasp. All of which has pushed me to the point where if I hear one more sarcastic comment from your rosebud lips, my dear, I intend to do something about it.'

'Oh.' Damaris felt his firm fingers curl softly round the nape of her neck, and then they were tangled in the short waves of her hair, pulling it a little too tightly.

She didn't ask what kind of 'something' he had in mind.

Instead, after a long pause during which the air

between them sparked with an almost visible tension, she said quietly, 'All right. You have a point.'

'I've certainly reached one.'

Damaris tried again. 'Joel, this time I'm *not* being sarcastic. But you *were* incredibly supercilious last night. And it seemed to me that you purposely staged that message calling you out because you wanted to get away from a scene you found tedious and beneath you. I wasn't impressed. Then you phoned me up today after I'd told you not to bother, and ordered me to fall smartly in line with your arrangements. You didn't even ask me. In fact you asked *Mary* whether or not I'd be busy.' She hesitated, fidgeting with the clasp on her bag. 'That may be the way you're used to handling your business associates, Joel Agar, but I've had enough men in my life who thought they owned me, and I'm not putting up with any more.' She gave the clasp one last, very decisive snap. 'What I *don't* understand is why you agreed to be the mystery guest in the first place if you found the whole thing such a terrible bore. And I especially don't see why you couldn't accept the easy way out I gave you.'

'Hmm.' Joel's eyes were hooded when she stole a glance at him, but his hand was stroking her neck quite gently now, and she found his touch startlingly pleasant. No, more than pleasant. It was—exhilarating.

'I see,' he said softly. 'All right, provided you behave yourself from now on I think I may let you off the hook. This time.'

'You'll what? Of all the arrogant. . .' She stopped because she saw that he was laughing. 'What's so funny?'

'You are,' he said, with an oddly soft look in his eyes. 'If you didn't make it so easy to tease you, I might not do it.'

Damaris glared at him again, quite speechless, and he laughed, then sobered quickly. 'I'm sorry,' he said. 'And of course you're quite right. Partly right at any rate. Will you listen without spitting in my eye if I try to explain?'

'I don't spit,' replied Damaris with dignity.

'Well, that's something. Then promise not to sting me either, wasp.'

'I'll *try*,' she said, forcing herself not to bare her teeth.

'Good.' He turned away from her to stare broodingly out of the window. 'You see, when I was originally asked to be the masked mystery my immediate reaction was to refuse. Emphatically. Not that I think there's anything intrinsically wrong with the raffle idea. It's a way of raising money for a cause which I happen to believe in. For good reason. But it's also the sort of undignified exhibition I don't care for. I'm used to being in the public eye, naturally. But as a businessman—not as some ridiculous male. . .'

'Stud?' suggested Damaris without thinking.

'You have a succinct way of putting things,' he observed drily. 'Yes. Precisely. Believe it or not, I prefer to keep my private life private. The prospect of being giggled over, not just by a bunch of society feather-brains but quite possibly by the gentlemen and ladies of the Press, had about as much appeal as—well, let's just say it held no appeal whatsoever.'

Damaris nodded. She could certainly identify with that. She had made a point of boycotting the article about last night's event when she had noticed it in the morning paper, but she hadn't been able to avoid a glimpse of the blown-up picture of the two of them holding hands and attempting to size each other up. The caption underneath began with the words, 'Will it be Love—or Hate?'

'What made you change your mind?' she asked him, with so much sympathy in her voice that Joel glanced at her with suspicion.

'Conscience, I suppose,' he said finally, when he saw that the sympathy was real. 'That—and memories. They couldn't get anyone else to do it. Or so they said. No one suitable.'

Oh, yes, and Joel had been suitable all right, thought Damaris. If he hadn't been, she wouldn't be sitting here feeling waves of disconcerting excitement every time his knee brushed up against her thigh.

'I guess I can understand that,' she murmured, wondering what he meant about memories. 'But once you'd agreed to do it——'

'Once I'd agreed to do it, why didn't I behave with better grace? Is that what you were going to ask me?'

'Well—yes.'

His wonderfully seductive lips curled wryly. 'I should have, of course. In fact I intended to. But when I found myself up there in front of that crowd of eager-eyed, predatory females—at least that's how they seemed to me—would you believe I wanted to turn around and run?'

'No,' said Damaris.

'I didn't think so. All the same, I didn't enjoy it.' His eyes mocked her. 'I suppose you wouldn't believe I'm shy, either?'

Damaris thought of all the stories she'd read about his business deals, and the hard-hitting speeches he'd made, and the ruthless but effective way he chaired meetings—not to mention the self-confident ease with which he'd got *her* to do his bidding.

'No,' she said. 'I wouldn't.'

He sighed. 'How about reserved, an essentially private

person who enjoys the company of women as individuals, but *not* when he's faced with a whole room full of them and begins to feel as if he's being served up as a prime cut of meat for dinner?'

'Beef,' said Damaris decidedly—and then put her hand over her face to hide a blush.

'How flattering,' he murmured, not looking at her.

She peered at him between her fingers, and, although not a muscle of his face seemed to be moving, there was something about his profile that made her think he was laughing at her—again.

'All right,' she said quickly. 'I do believe that much. I mean about your not enjoying that sort of thing.'

'Do you, now? And do you also believe that I behaved as well as a prime cut can possibly be expected to behave—in the circumstances?'

Damaris giggled. She couldn't help it. 'I—I guess so.'

'Good.'

'But,' she added severely, 'that's no excuse for arranging to be called away. Or for arranging this evening without asking me.'

'On the first point you're absolutely right. It seemed a good idea at the time, but I agree with you that it was inexcusable—and I apologise. On the second point. . .' He turned to face her and grinned suddenly. 'On the second point, you're absolutely wrong. If I'd asked you instead of telling you, or if I'd given you sufficient time to think, you wouldn't have come. Would you?'

'No-o,' admitted Damaris, unable to lie while Joel's eyes were on her, hypnotising her into telling him the truth.

'That's what I thought.'

'Yes—but why should you want me to come with you?

You've already made it clear you don't like that kind of fund raising.'

'I don't. But that doesn't mean I don't like you.'

'I can't see any reason why you should.'

'Neither can I. Let's say you piqued my interest. After all, I expected a giddy little social butterfly. Instead I was confronted by—a wasp.'

'Oh,' said Damaris. 'I get it. You're not used to women who don't fall all over you, so it was necessary to your ego to prove that I'm as vulnerable as the rest of my sex.'

Before she even knew what was happening to her, Joel's arm had snaked around her shoulders, and she was pulled up hard against his chest.

'You just don't learn, do you, Damaris?' he murmured with a soft kind of menace. 'I don't know about vulnerable, my dear, but you're certainly extremely discourteous—and very foolish. I thought I told you that any further sarcasm from you would be summarily dealt with.'

His full lips were just above her own, which had parted in surprise—and something else—as she felt his hard male warmth against her breasts.

'I—I. . .' she started to stutter.

'You, my dear, are just about to be kissed.'

Damaris tried to struggle, but his arm only tightened across her back. And then she stopped struggling because his mouth was pressed against hers, forcing it open, and she found that she couldn't breathe, let alone fight him. It was as much as she could do to prevent herself from melting completely, from giving in to something that she had known instinctively, from the moment she first saw that masked cut-out across the

ballroom, was going to be trouble. The kind of trouble
that could easily overturn all the careful decisions she
had made after Scott died, when she had vowed never to
get involved with a man again.

Now she sat rigidly in Joel's embrace, her fists
clenched tight against his chest, forcing herself not to
respond to him, not to let her arms wind round his neck.

His tongue probed deeper and she made a small sound
in her throat, her lips opening to receive him in spite of
herself. Because his kiss wasn't hard or punishing. It
was warm, insidious, stirring needs she'd forgotten she
had—and the touch of his hand moving gently over the
thin gold fabric at her shoulders was an aphrodisiac,
drugging, impossible to resist. . .

Slowly her fists unclenched as her palms spread out
against his shirt.

And then it was over, abruptly, as if it had never
happened, and Joel was saying briskly as he switched on
the engine of the car, 'Did you say something about not
being vulnerable to my somewhat debatable charms? I
hope that's cured you of any further sarcasm, my dear.
At least for the moment. And in case you were wondering, I wouldn't have dreamed of arranging a date with a
woman who said she wasn't interested in me—there *are*
one or two, you know—if I hadn't been very sure she
was lying through her teeth.'

'Bastard,' said Damaris.

Joel smiled cynically. 'Can't you do better than that?'

She could, but at the moment she didn't see the point.
Because he was right. She didn't like him; in fact she
positively detested him most of the time. But she *was*
quite fatally attracted to him. And she didn't know what
to do about it.

'I think you'd better take me home,' she said, her eyes on the road as Joel sped away from the kerb.

'Certainly not.'

'But—you can't want to take me to dinner now.'

'Why ever not? I quite enjoyed the hors d'oeuvres. As far as I'm concerned, the evening can only get better.'

'Don't count on it,' said Damaris morosely, and then relapsed into a brooding silence.

She was so lost in her own thoughts that she didn't notice where they were going until she realised that the Jaguar was slowing down to pull into a car park. At the bottom of a mountain. Grouse Mountain.

She choked back a gasp. If only she'd asked him earlier where they were going, she could surely have persuaded him in time to change his plans. As it was now, she was faced with two alternatives. She could create a ridiculous scene and insist that he take her home at once. Or she could hold her breath for the next fifteen minutes and hope that Joel didn't notice that she'd turned into a quivering, neurotic jelly. Just for the moment it seemed important to retain what shreds of dignity she had left. But she wasn't sure she could do it. Because she knew now where Joel intended to take her, and it meant that they would have to glide up the side of that mountain in a glassed-in gondola suspended high above the steep, tree-lined slopes. And then they would dine in the famous restaurant with the famous view, perched three-thousand seven-hundred feet above Vancouver.

And she was deathly afraid of heights.

CHAPTER THREE

'COME along, out you get.' Joel was holding the car door open, waiting for Damaris to move.

'I—um—aren't we terribly late?' she stalled. 'I mean, perhaps they haven't held your reservation.'

Joel's thick eyebrows rose dauntingly. 'They've held it,' he said in the sort of tone she imagined he used on his staff when they displeased him.

Yes, of course they'd held it. It was inconceivable that the successful and powerful Joel Agar should have to arrive on time like other mortals.

She eased herself slowly out of the seat and he took her arm lightly, a slight frown between his thickly arched eyebrows.

'Is something wrong?' he asked curtly. 'Other than your natural inclination to provoke me?'

That did it. There was no way she was going to let this arrogant man know she was afraid. It was only a short ride to the top of the lift and she would just have to grit her teeth and bear it. Once they got to the restaurant she would be all right.

'Nothing's wrong,' she replied loftily. 'Shall we go?'

Joel's only answer was to increase the pressure on her arm and lead her smartly up the steps to the waiting gondola.

A few minutes later, staring straight ahead up the mountain so that she wouldn't have to watch the city as it dropped away behind them, they were swinging across the car park with a dozen other passengers. As far as Damaris was concerned, they were on their way to hell.

Joel released her arm once they were aboard, and with nothing solid to hold on to she gazed glassily up the steep slope. The gondola didn't sway much—perhaps if she closed her eyes. . . Yes, she could cope with it this way. . .

Then she gasped, and the breath was smashed from her body as the conveyance jerked and bumped its way past the first of the two support towers. Her stomach rose up to meet her throat as her eyes flew open and she grabbed frantically at the first thing that came to hand— in this case Joel's manly arm.

He glanced down at her, surprised that for once she was making what seemed to be a friendly overture. Then his eyes narrowed.

'You've gone a most repulsive shade of green,' he informed her. 'What's the matter?'

'N—nothing.'

'Nonsense. Aren't you well?'

'I'm f—fine.' Her grip on his arm became desperate as they approached the second tower, and suddenly Joel got the picture.

'Oh, no. You're afraid of heights, aren't you?'

Damaris nodded, beyond speech now as her knees buckled beneath her. She saw Joel frown, was sure he had completely lost patience with her, and found she was past caring what he thought. Then his strong arm was around her shoulders, holding her close against his side, supporting her so that she couldn't fall.

'It's all right,' he said, quite kindly. 'You're safe with me, Damaris. And don't worry—we're almost there.'

To her amazement, and for the first time in many years, she did feel safe and secure, in spite of being suspended above the ground—and a moment later, just as Joel had promised, they had reached the top and were alighting from the terrifying contraption.

'You should have told me,' he reproved her. 'I'm not a complete brute, you know. I wouldn't have made you come up here if I'd known.'

'I didn't want you to think I was a coward.' She sighed, still shaking. 'Although the truth is I'm a total chicken.'

'I doubt it. Everyone's afraid of something. It took courage even to attempt it, feeling the way you do.'

He was actually being nice to her. In spite of all the awful things she'd said to him. And he had said everyone was afraid of something. She wondered what *he* was afraid of, but at the moment she was having enough trouble dealing with her own fear, so she didn't ask.

'Come on, you need to sit down and have something strengthening to drink,' he told her, hustling her across an open space between the gondola and an attractive fir and cedar chalet.

By the time they reached the security of the elegantly appointed dining-room, with its antiqued chairs, wooden pillars, and warmly opulent black, red and gold décor, Damaris's nerves were almost under control.

'Do you mind sitting by the window?' he asked as an afterthought, as they were shown through glass doors to a table for two which, to Damaris's stunned gaze, appeared to overlook half the world.

'No, I'm fine as long as there's solid ground underneath me,' she replied, still transfixed by the magnificent panorama of Vancouver stretching out for miles far below them, and thinking that if it hadn't been for Joel she might never have seen this breathtakingly lovely scene.

'Good.' He helped her into her chair and in the next instant, as if by magic, a large glass of brandy appeared in front of her.

'But I hardly ever drink anything—except a little wine sometimes,' she protested.

'Don't argue. Just do as you're told and drink up.'

She was still too weak and emotionally exhausted to do more than glare at him, before doing exactly as he ordered.

When he saw that her cheeks had returned to their normal colour—soft rose instead of sea-green—he asked quietly, but as if he meant to have an answer, 'What makes you so afraid, Damaris? Have you always been like that?'

The setting sun glowed and hid her eyes, which were fastened on a nameless bird dozing sleepily on a rock outside the window. 'More or less.'

'I see.' He was silent for a moment. 'You're not telling me the whole truth, are you?'

She hesitated. He was right, of course, but she wasn't sure she wanted to tell him the truth. Even if he was being nice to her for a change. On the other hand, he wasn't the sort of man one lied to either.

'No,' she admitted reluctantly. 'Not the whole truth.'

'Sometimes, if you talk about things, you find the fear goes away,' he suggested, his crooked smile calm and reassuring.

'Not this fear,' said Damaris, with such conviction that his smile faded.

'I see.'

'No, you don't.' He was looking disbelieving and superior again, and suddenly, wanting to shock him, she said baldly, 'When I was seven my foster-father got drunk one evening—he got drunk a lot of evenings, but this was different—and he threw me out of the upper-storey bedroom I shared with his two daughters. I landed in a flower bed, and it was so unexpected that my body went completely limp. All I got was a few bruises——'

Joel's amber-brown eyes turned diamond hard. 'And he got a gaol term, I hope?'

'Oh, no. My social worker never found out she'd made a mistake when she placed me with the family. I was too scared to tell her. But that time my foster-mother got scared too and she must have said something to my father to make him listen, because he never did it again. I was punished a lot, but always within the limits of the law.'

'Why were you punished?' His voice grated harshly, and she looked up, startled.

'I'm not sure. Sometimes I suppose I'd done something, but half the time I didn't know what it was. The truth, I think, was that I was a nuisance to them. They applied for a foster-child because they thought the money would help them feed their own six kids. It *didn't* help much, but they still kept me, and pretended they wanted me. It wouldn't have looked good to their friends if they'd given me up, and that mattered to my foster-father. He liked being thought of as a social benefactor.'

'Hmm.' Joel's fingers curled round the stem of his glass, thick lashes shielding his eyes. When he finally looked at her his expression had altered, and somehow she knew he had just fought, and won, a battle to control an almost overwhelming anger. 'I'm beginning to understand why the angel turned into a wasp,' he said, his voice betraying no particular emotion. Then he smiled slightly. 'On the other hand, perhaps your unpleasant guardian was merely trying to cure your tongue of its unfortunate propensity for acid.'

Damaris knew he was teasing her this time, attempting to add some lightness to an atmosphere which had turned unexpectedly sombre.

'I expect he was,' she agreed demurely, responding to his smile and pulling a face.

'Wasp,' he murmured, almost affectionately now.

Their meal came then, and they didn't speak of her childhood again until much later.

The food was wonderful. Rack of lamb for him and steamed halibut Grand Marnier for her, followed by mocha fudge tart and fresh fruit kebabs for dessert, all served with unobtrusive efficiency by a well-trained staff. She hadn't had food like this since Scott had first taken her out, she reflected wistfully.

They made small talk during most of the meal, at ease with each other now that her fear of heights had somehow broken the ice. They discussed the view, and they found that they had the odd mutual acquaintance because Scott and Joel had sometimes moved in the same circles, and, although Damaris had attended few social functions with her husband, some of his business had been conducted at home. Joel was surprised to learn that she was the widow of a man he had known reasonably well at one time.

It wasn't until the coffee came, and the night began to sparkle with distant lights, that they returned to the subject of Damaris's early years.

'I know I have no right to ask,' he said, looking her straight in the eye, 'but you've made me realise how secure my own childhood was, compared to yours. I didn't always appreciate that at the time.' He smiled, a nice, sympathetic smile. 'What happened to your birth parents, Damaris?'

'My mother died when I was six. Of malnutrition and just plain bad management, I think.'

There. That should shut him up. She didn't want to talk about her past.

Joel's mouth hardened. 'I'm sorry. I shouldn't have asked.'

'It's all right.' Now she felt guilty that she'd been abrupt. 'Mother always managed to feed me somehow,' she told him reluctantly, 'but I don't think she cared much about herself after my father left her. They weren't legally married in any case, and he never sent her any support.'

'Is he still alive?'

'I don't know.'

'Or care,' he said. It was a statement, not a question, and for some reason his perception surprised her.

'Or care,' she agreed. 'Any more than he did. Or does.'

'Mm. So then you were put in the foster home, I suppose.'

'Yes. I was there until I was sixteen. My foster-father died then, and my foster-mother went to pieces. So I left home, moved from Quillville—it's a small Interior town you'll never have heard of—and found work in a flower shop here in Vancouver. I was glad to go.'

'I can imagine,' he replied, staring grimly into his coffee. When he lifted his head she saw that he was about to frame another question, and quickly changed the subject.

'And you? You had a contented and—and profitable childhood?'

He choked into his cup. 'You *do* have a way with words. I don't know about profitable, but yes, I was contented. I was also the eldest of four children and I guess you could say we were poor but happy. Quite a cliché, in fact.'

'Not any more,' said Damaris. 'You're hardly a cliché these days, are you? Or was it a matter of rags to riches?'

'Not rags. Good, serviceable clothing.'

Damaris smiled, her eyes running over the expensive suit and the gold cuff-links and watch. 'Circumstances change, don't they?' she murmured.

'Fortunately. They appear to have changed in your case too.' His gaze rested broodingly on her topaz necklace and earrings, and then he asked abruptly, 'What's the "C" for?'

Damaris blinked. 'The "C"?'

'In "C Damaris Gordon".'

'Oh.' She laughed self-consciously. 'How did you know about that?'

'It was on the ticket that brought us together. Remember?' His deep-set eyes glimmered at her in the warm light coming from the lowered ceiling.

Damaris gulped the last of her brandy. 'It's for "Charity",' she said at last, staring fixedly at a point above his tie.

'Charity?' He laughed softly. 'Well, I'm damned. In view of the way we met, highly appropriate. Why did you change it?'

She raised her eyes resolutely to meet his. 'Because I got tired of being asked where Faith and Hope were. Besides—the word charity hit a bit too close to home. When I started at the flower shop I changed it. To my second name.'

'Mm. Makes sense. It's a pretty name.'

'Yes,' she said—and then, suddenly tired of explanations, she added brightly, 'You can use it if you like—instead of wasp.'

He laughed. '*Touché*. Mind you, there are other options. I've been tempted to use several of them this evening.'

'Such as?' she demanded, the light of battle sparking in her eye.

'How do you feel about CD?'

'Negative,' she replied shortly, knowing that that wasn't what he'd had in mind at all.

'Very well, then we'll settle for Damaris, shall we?'

'It means "gentle as a kitten",' she informed him smugly. It wasn't true, but his reaction should be interesting.

Joel choked for the second time that evening. 'In that case I vote for CD.'

Damaris contemplated throwing the rest of her coffee at him, but she was enjoying it so she stuck out her tongue instead.

Joel's eyes gleamed. 'Very alluring,' he mocked her. 'You, my dear, are proving much more of a challenge than I expected.'

'And you're proving much more of a. . .' She had been going to say, 'more of a bastard.' But it wasn't true. He was proving much nicer than she had expected. And, although she wouldn't have believed it possible, much sexier.

That thought brought her up short.

'More of a problem,' she finished quickly.

'I'm glad to hear it. And at this stage I don't think I'll ask what you mean.'

That was just as well, because at this stage she didn't have an answer to give him.

Twenty minutes later, secure in the circle of his arms, Damaris stood on the observation platform watching the lights of the city wink on and off in the distance.

'It's lovely,' she said after a while. 'I'm glad I came.'

'Yes,' he agreed quietly, 'so am I. Do you feel brave enough to ride back now?'

To her surprise she did, and not long afterwards, with her head held firmly against Joel's chest and her face pressed into the darkness of his jacket, the gondola swung them gently down the mountain. Once or twice she even found the courage to peek over her shoulder at the city, rising up fast now to greet them.

In no time at all, it seemed, they had reached the bottom, and now for the first time Damaris noticed the tall woman stepping on to the platform in front of them. Her left eye was almost swollen shut and the skin around it was coloured an ugly purple. She walked very stiffly and the man beside her, silver-haired and distinguished, was looking at her with a curious kind of triumph.

'*He* did that to her,' said Damaris later, as they climbed into the car and began to fasten their seatbelts.

'What?' Joel looked startled. 'Oh, I doubt it. She probably got smashed in a car accident.'

'Oh, no, she didn't. I know the signs.'

'Do you?' he said, backing the car up with one hand, and not paying much attention. 'I haven't a lot of patience with women who put up with that sort of thing. It's gutless.'

Damaris glowered at him, but he was concentrating on the road and didn't see her.

'What the hell do you think you know about it?' she snapped, when he didn't seem inclined to pursue the subject. '*You* weren't abused as a child and then married too young to a man who gave you six children in six years, so that you were too tired and too dependent on him to think straight. And even when you did get a chance to think, you knew you had no skills and six kids

to look after, who might get taken away from you if you
blew the whistle. Even if they weren't, you wouldn't be
able to support them. It's easy for you, with all your
money and influence and surrounded by everything you
need, to sit there condemning those women for putting
up with it. And they shouldn't, of course. But you've
never had to live through it.'

'Neither have you.' Joel sounded more bored than
angry.

'No, but my foster-mother did. That's why she never
had time to do more than feed and clothe me—a seventh
child who wasn't even her own.'

He didn't say anything for a long time, and she began
to think he hadn't been listening. Then, as he swung the
Jaguar expertly round a bend, he said without looking at
her, 'I apologise. That was thoughtless of me. You're
right, of course.'

Oh, yes, she was right. She didn't need him to tell her
that. But somehow the evening, which had turned out so
much better than she'd expected, was soured now,
because she had also been right about Joel. He was too
sure of himself, too complacent, too successful—and too
damned rich—to have much compassion for those who,
it must seem to him, brought most of their problems on
themselves. What was more, he was in his late thirties
now, she supposed, and not at all likely to change.

'It doesn't matter,' she said tiredly.

He glanced at her sharply, then turned away again, his
strong jaw protruding hard and square.

They drove the rest of the way back to her house in a
strained silence.

'Thank you for the evening,' she said coolly as she
stood on the step with her back to him, rifling through
her bag for the key.

She felt his hand on her shoulder. 'Aren't you going to ask me in, Damaris?'

'No,' she said, pulling out the key and clutching it as if it were a lifeline. 'I'd rather not.'

'Really. I wonder why that is?'

His hand was still on her shoulder and she could feel his wine-warm breath on her cheek. She started to turn the key in the lock, but the moment she did so his grip tightened and he swung her smartly around so that she found herself staring at his chest. No wonder he seemed taller than he was, she thought irrelevantly. Next to him, even in heels, there wasn't a whole lot of her.

'What——?' she began.

'I want to kiss you,' he said matter-of-factly. 'Last time I didn't ask you. This time I am.'

'Oh,' she said, swallowing, her eyes still fixed well below his chin. 'I—I don't think that's a good idea.'

'I don't see why not. I rather enjoyed it the first time. So did you.'

'I—um—yes, I did.' There wasn't much point in denying it. 'But as we won't be seeing each other again, it would seem—hypocritical.'

'Oh, would it? And what makes you think we won't be seeing each other again?'

'But—you only owed me one date.'

'So I've paid my debt. Now I'd like to take you out because I choose to. Not because I feel I have to.'

'Oh.' Damaris's hand flew to the topaz necklace, twisting it against her pale skin. 'I—no. Thank you. I'm flattered. But I *don't* choose to.'

'I see.'

She couldn't make out his features clearly because she'd forgotten to turn the porch light on, but she didn't need to see to know he was angry. Not used to being turned down, she thought with an unworthy feeling of triumph.

'So I'm still a monster, am I?' he asked bleakly.

'No, of course not. It's just that——'

'That I put my foot in it when I made that remark about the woman with the purple eye. Aren't I allowed one mistake?'

'Of course. It's not just that.' It wasn't, but a lot of it was, and she spoke more coldly than she intended.

Joel had both hands on her shoulders now, and one of them moved round to the back of her neck. 'You certainly know how to hold a grudge, don't you?' he said, dispassionately. 'One day I'll have to teach you how to forgive—as well as how to behave. You could use a few lessons, Mrs Gordon.'

'You're not teaching me anything,' hissed Damaris, wondering if Jane Spencer was on the other side of the door. 'Goodnight, Mr Agar.'

Joel's fingers moved to her chin, exerting a gentle pressure, and she found her mouth tilted up to his.

'Goodnight, wasp,' he replied equably. His thumb traced her lower lip in a lingering exploration, before his mouth descended to touch hers, very briefly, and with such intoxicating sweetness that she was left hungering hopelessly for more. For more of him.

He stepped back, let his eyes play speculatively over the outline of her delicate figure, and without another word disappeared silently beneath the shadows thrown by the trees.

The moment the door shut behind her she heard the Jaguar start up and purr smoothly away into the night.

As the stillness of the house closed around her, Damaris collapsed against the wall and closed her eyes. What was it Joel had said about *asking* if he could kiss her this time? Well, he hadn't asked. On the other hand, she was bound to admit with a pang of unwelcome regret, he hadn't really kissed her either.

Damn. She had gone with him tonight specifically in order to get him off her mind, sure that his domineering arrogance would cure her of any burgeoning infatuation far more quickly than her craven refusal to see him. But it hadn't worked.

In some ways she liked him better than she had at first. He'd been kind about her fear of heights, and sympathetic when he'd learned the circumstances of her childhood. That was surprising too, come to think of it. If anyone had suggested earlier that she would end up talking to Joel about her past, she would have laughed in their face. But this wasn't funny.

Sure, she liked Joel better now. She was also incredibly attracted to him. But the fact remained that he had no real understanding of those who were less successful and less aggressively confident than himself. She knew from what she'd read about him that he had built his car empire with a brilliant blend of business acumen, ruthlessness, and the cool conviction that anyone could have anything they wanted if they worked for it. And although he was reputed to be scrupulously honest that didn't mean he had any tolerance for human inefficiency or weakness. His attitude to the unfortunate woman on the gondola had demonstrated that all too clearly.

He didn't like kids or cats either, and those particular aversions would win him no brownie points with her.

A door opened quietly and Damaris returned to the world around her—specifically the world of babysitters wanting to go home.

'You're back,' said Jane, almost accusingly. 'I didn't hear you come in.'

She *hadn't* been listening then, thought Damaris. Thank goodness for that. 'I expect you had the TV on,' she replied mildly, handing over her payment for the evening. 'Thank you, Jane.'

She watched as the girl crossed the road and disappeared through the back gate to her house, which was visible from the end of the cul-de-sac. Then she walked slowly into the television room, switched off the set—it was showing a lurid love story she was sure Jane wasn't meant to watch—and sank down into her favourite deep armchair.

What an evening, she thought numbly. But at least it was over, and since she'd been anything but encouraging to Joel he probably wouldn't call her any more. She'd seen plenty of pictures of the glamorous ladies he was usually seen escorting, and she certainly wasn't in their class. On the other hand, he wasn't the first man who'd found her passably attractive. Before Scott there had been Craig. He'd worked in the accounting department of Gordon and Son's Insurance, which was where she had been employed after taking a typing course at night school and leaving her job at the flower shop. Eventually there had been Scott Gordon himself, the president's son.

She touched her necklace again, needing its hard reality. Yes, there had been Scott. But there was no doubt that she had seen the last of Joel.

Upstairs Ginny murmured in her sleep, and Damaris jumped up to make sure that all was well. Her daughter's curly blonde head was down at the bottom of the cot, and she was curled on her side with her thumb planted firmly in her mouth. Damaris smiled and pulled a pink blanket up around the sleeping baby. Then she tiptoed quietly to her own room to get herself ready for bed.

'Meow-rr,' protested Candy as her mistress slipped under the covers.

'Sorry, Candy,' she muttered, 'but in case you hadn't noticed, this is *my* bed.'

Candy's only reply was to dig her white-tipped paws possessively into the blankets.

Damaris lay back on the pillows, sure she wouldn't be able to fall asleep. But in just a few minutes she was dreaming—of a man with wide, amber-brown eyes and lips that were too seductive to be real. . .a man who, when he had forgotten to liken her to a wasp, had called her a baby angel.

And she hadn't seen the last of him at all.

The first rose came the next day. A perfect, pale yellow bud that looked as if the dew still clung to its delicate petals. There was a note attached to it. All it said was, 'Whatever I've done, forgive me. Only elephants and wasps hold grudges.' There was no signature.

That's all he knows, thought Damaris, who needed no signature to recognise the source of that message. He should have tried living with *my* family. Or Scott, for that matter.

After the rose, which was beautiful but not exactly extravagant for a man who must be worth millions, she expected Joel would call her that night. But he didn't, and the next day two more roses came, pale pink this time and equally perfect—but with no note or explanation.

The following day three roses came, deep red and glowing like rubies. But still no further note or phone call.

The fourth and fifth days brought more roses, each time a different colour, and on the sixth day six roses were delivered, all creamy white. That made twenty-one roses in all, arranged about the living-room in glass vases. Surely he would phone today. Then, of course, she would have to tell him that although she loved the flowers she really couldn't see him again.

She'd thought about that very carefully in the clear light of the morning after, and she'd come to the half regretful conclusion that although she too liked challenges she had no intention of getting involved with a man again, and so it wouldn't be fair to either of them to take their acquaintance any further. Besides, if she ever changed her mind about involvement, she certainly wouldn't choose a man who disliked cats and children and had no patience at all with those less assertive than himself.

On the ninth day the roses were still coming, and Damaris could stand it no longer.

'What's going on, Chloe?' she demanded of her neighbour, as she stamped across next door that evening carrying a fussily indignant Ginny who had just been sharply dissuaded from sharing her dinner with the cat. 'He keeps sending me roses, but he never comes near me. Surely he doesn't expect me to call *him*?'

'No, because he knows damn well you'd never get through to him,' replied Chloe. 'His home number is sure to be unlisted, and he'll have an army of secretaries screening his calls at work. I bet he hopes you'll try though. It looks to me as if he's trying to get you rattled. Then when you're totally distracted, he'll move in for the kill.'

'Kill?' croaked Damaris. 'Now wait a minute. . .'

'You know what I mean. He wants to get you into bed, surely?'

Ginny created a welcome diversion at that point by

emptying a tray full of Chloe's jewellery on to the floor, and by the time it was all gathered up again—no easy feat in view of all the other debris on the carpet— Damaris was once again composed.

'I don't know,' she replied, with pretended indifference. 'I really can't imagine why he should. Anyway, he's out of luck if you're right because I'm not getting anywhere near his bed.'

'Suit yourself.' Chloe shrugged. 'I'll have him if you don't want him. I could do with a brief encounter at the moment. It's been a month since I broke up with Frank.'

'I thought that was Clinton.'

'No, Clinton was the month before that.'

'Oh.' Damaris gave up. Then she added reluctantly, not sure why the idea annoyed her, 'I suppose you can have Joel if you want him—and if you can get him.'

'I was only kidding.' Chloe laughed. 'He'd be much too pig-headed and particular for me. Listen, if you want to know what's going on why don't you ask Mary? He talked to her before, didn't he? When he wanted to know what you were doing?'

'He wouldn't. . .' began Damaris. Then she stopped. How did she know what he wouldn't do? All the same, she was damned if she'd give Mary the opportunity to meddle any more than she had already. Mary Carmichael had done quite enough damage as it was.

'I'll think about it,' she said non-committally. 'Thanks, Chloe. I'd better be going now. I think Ginny's about to eat your slippers.'

'How unappetising,' murmured Chloe with a shudder. 'It doesn't matter, though. I never wear them.'

Damaris shook her head, and left her friend's house grinning widely. It was wonderful how half an hour of Chloe's company could be counted on to cure her of the blues—even if she still had no idea what to do about the roses. She could write to thank Joel, of course, but he might take that as encouragement. . .

Maybe Chloe ought to have him after all. No man could ever get the better of that self-confident individualist for long. . .

"'On the Twelfth Day of Christmas,'" warbled Damaris three days later, when yet another box arrived from the flower shop. This time the roses were a soft peach, their petals finely tipped with dark pink. Only it wasn't Christmas, was it? It was springtime, and she'd just received a dozen beautiful roses. A dozen. Surely that had to have some significance. Today, at last, she might reasonably expect some overture from Joel.

But no overture was made and when, the next day, no flowers came either, Damaris was forced to re-examine her feelings. Much more honestly than she had been inclined to do up until this point. And the truth was, she was horribly disappointed. There was no getting away from it. She desperately wanted to hear from Joel again and maybe, after all, she didn't mean to turn him down. Which was crazy, because she was perfectly contented living here with Ginny. Scott had left her more than comfortably off, and since she had sold her shares in his company she was no longer obliged to hold a job. For the first time in her life she was completely independent, free from worries about money. Why should she want to complicate this ideal situation? She thought about that. Of course, the fact of the matter was, she didn't want to. But more or less against her will she was being drawn into something that was totally outside her experience.

'Maybe this is bigger than both of us,' she grumbled to Candy, who twitched her long marmalade tail with haughty indifference and padded off into the garden.

'You're right,' Damaris called after her. 'Who am I kidding? Joel has had an amusing little game that he's tired of, and I'm suffering from a childish attack of dudgeon mixed in with long-delayed and very juvenile hormones.'

She sighed, kicked irritably at a rubber ball belonging to Ginny, and ten minutes later was on the phone to Mary.

'Joel Agar?' repeated Mary in her most mellifluously county voice. 'Yes, as a matter of fact I did run into him at some charity function. Now let me see, when would that have been?'

She knows quite well when it was, thought Damaris. If I haven't learned to recognise Mary's evasions by now, I never will.

'Did you have some particular reason for asking?' her neighbour enquired; and then, lowering her voice to a puzzlingly uncharacteristic whisper, she added, 'I understood you disapproved of Mr Agar, Damaris. It was a great disappointment to me.'

Damaris gritted her teeth. 'I don't disapprove of him,' she said levelly. 'It's just that he's been sending me roses, and I don't quite know what to do about them.'

'Thank him, I should think,' replied Mary, as if she were talking to a particularly stupid child.

'Yes, but I haven't seen him. I wondered if——'

'You can write to him then.' Mary had never had any inhibitions about interrupting, but at this moment she sounded positively rude, as if she was anxious to get rid of her caller.

'I suppose I could.' There was no way that Damaris was telling her bossy neighbour that she was damned if she was making the first move. In a sense it wouldn't be, of course, as Joel *had* sent the roses, but. . .

'Thanks, Mary,' she murmured. 'It doesn't matter.'

If Mary knew anything at all about Joel's activities, she certainly wasn't letting on.

Damaris wandered into the kitchen and stared moodily at the lunch dishes, which she'd left piled all over the sink instead of stacking them tidily in the dishwasher as was her habit. Heavens, if this kept up she'd be getting as bad as Chloe. And that wouldn't do.

She had just placed the last plate in the machine when she thought she heard the front door opening. She paused, frozen, but there was no further sound so she decided she must have imagined it and started to close the lid. It wouldn't shut.

'Damn,' she snapped, wrestling it open again and bending over to rearrange the guilty saucepan. She slammed it down over a tray of knives and forks with an impatient mutter, and grumbled under her breath, 'This is ridiculous.'

'It is a little,' agreed a deep male voice from the doorway. 'Very attractive though. In fact, if I may say so, extremely tempting.'

CHAPTER FOUR

FOR a moment Damaris felt as if she had been turned to stone, sculpted in this undignified position with her jeans-clad bottom pointed neatly up in the air. Then, as an incredible warmth began to creep through her body, she straightened slowly, knowing whom she would see when she turned around. Only a few minutes ago she had been longing for the sound of his voice, but now that he was actually here she couldn't decide whether she wanted him to drop through the floor and stay there, or whether she wanted to drop through it herself.

Joel took one look at her face, grimaced and said ruefully, 'Mm. Bad timing. Would you like me to go out and start again? I promise to make a lot more noise the next time.'

Damaris stared at him. He was wearing a beige pullover under a battered brown leather jacket, and he didn't look nearly as formidable as she remembered. In fact he looked sexy and appealing and almost boyish. Her stomach curled up and turned a somersault before it made a nose-dive for her knees.

He was grinning now, and she knew her face still resembled a boiled beetroot. 'Don't be absurd,' she mumbled. 'What are you doing here? And how in the world did you get in?'

'To answer your second question first, I was visiting Mary Carmichael when you called. She mentioned that your other neighbour—a scatter-brained lady in a hair-band, sneakers and very little else—had your key in case of emergencies. Incidentally, the incomparable Mary is quite put out that you didn't put *her* in charge of all possible crises.'

'That'll be the frosty Friday morning,' scoffed Damaris, her colour beginning to fade at last. Then she had a sudden vision of Chloe in a hairband and sneakers, entertaining Joel in her front hall. 'I bet Chloe was put out too if you walked in on her when she had no clothes on,' she added drily.

'Ah, but I didn't. She opened the door quite voluntarily, wrapped in what appeared to be a see-through curtain.'

'It probably was, knowing Chloe. How did you persuade her to let you have my key?'

'I said it was an emergency and she believed me.'

'Like hell she did,' Damaris muttered.

This cul-de-sac was becoming a positive hotbed of intrigue, she reflected—and apparently with only one end in mind: that of uniting her with Joel Agar. No doubt in more ways than one. She frowned, then gave herself a mental shake because Joel was looking at her with one raised eyebrow, and she knew this was no time to be plotting vengeance on her neighbours. She could deal with those conspirators later.

'Now that you're here,' she suggested with what she hoped was regal condescension, 'perhaps you'd care to sit down.'

'Perhaps I would.' He pulled out a chair from the table, swung it round and sat with his long legs stretched easily in front of him and his arms crossed loosely on his chest. 'Well,' he asked, cocking the other eyebrow at her, 'do you want me to answer your first question? Oh, and incidentally you have permission to sit in my presence.' He waved a lordly hand at a chair.

'Keep that up and you won't have permission to sit in my kitchen,' retorted Damaris. But she took the seat he had indicated and propped her elbows up on the table.

'Yes,' she said, 'I do want some answers. What *are* you doing here, Joel? Why couldn't you ring the bell like other people? And—why the roses?'

'It's usual to say "thank you for the roses". Not, "why the roses?"'

'Thank you for the roses,' she replied, with an edge to her voice. 'They're lovely. But they don't explain why you're here —or why you sent them.'

'All right.' He grinned wolfishly. 'I'll come clean. I sent them to soften you up. After our last encounter I was sure you'd turn me down if I asked you out. Short of kidnapping you, roses seemed the simplest solution.'

'But you didn't phone.'

'Of course not. I figured you'd be crazy with curiosity by this time. Confused and—more susceptible.'

'Susceptible to what?' she asked with deep suspicion.

'Me,' he replied smugly.

'You're not some kind of virus,' she snapped. 'And I'm not in the least susceptible.'

'Yes, you are. And I'm relieved to hear you regard me as at least one step above the common cold. By the way, I didn't ring the bell because I find that surprises are much more effective. In business as well as—other matters. It was a stroke of luck I happened to be next door when you phoned though.' He gazed innocently up at the ceiling.

'You didn't happen to be next door. I bet you were discussing tactics with Mary and the whole thing was some stupid plot. Although for the life of me I don't see why any of you bothered.'

He shrugged. 'Very well, I plead guilty. If you must

know, your friends bothered because, in their different ways, they both think your life needs livening up. Flatteringly, and perhaps misguidedly, they look on me as a likely candidate for the job. I bothered because——'

'I know,' said Damaris, morosely echoing Chloe's assumptions. 'You bothered because you want to get me into bed.'

Joel leaned back, put his hands behind his head and gave her a long and leisurely appraisal. 'It's a charming proposition,' he drawled, as her face turned from crimson to mottled purple, 'and of course I'd be delighted to oblige. . .' He bent forward suddenly, deep eyes seductively caressing. 'More than delighted. But I'm afraid the truth, as so often happens, is somewhat less inspiring. You see, I only came to ask you out to dinner. Though naturally if you'd prefer it——'

'I wouldn't prefer it,' said Damaris hastily. 'You know I didn't mean it that way.'

'I don't know anything of the sort,' he replied, and she knew he wasn't teasing her any more. 'You've admitted you enjoyed kissing me—not that I needed to be told—and you've been a widow for a year and a half now——'

'I see,' she interrupted with deadly softness. 'So you think I may be desperate for your—services? How much do you charge, Mr Agar?'

Joel swore, briefly and with proficiency, then rose to move purposefully around the table. She saw his knuckles, white against the maple, as he leaned over her, his face very close to her own.

'You don't really think you're getting away with that, do you?' His tone was almost conversational, but there was no way she could miss the threat behind his words.

She clutched the seat of her chair hard, with both hands. 'I—what are you going to do?' Her grey eyes, riveted on his, were wide and anxious. Whatever form or revenge he meant to take, she was alone in the house with a sleeping child and a cat. And Joel was a powerful and, at this moment, definitely angry man.

His gaze moved down to her clutching hands and his mouth twisted. 'That chair won't protect you at all if I decide to do what you're thinking,' he taunted her.

Damaris wasn't sure what she was thinking. From the direction his eyes were taking, she suspected she was about to get her bottom whacked. On the other hand, he had assured her he didn't believe in violence. . .and there was something very sexual, almost animal, about the way he was leaning over her now. Sensuality surged from him in waves. She ran her tongue over dry lips, aware that she was responding to the message his body was sending—and that if he moved so much as a finger towards her he was not likely to meet with much resistance. And the fact that she couldn't resist him had the effect of making her almost as angry as he was.

'Don't threaten me,' she warned him, by some miracle managing to keep her voice level.

'I never make threats unless I mean to carry them out,' he assured her, placing both large hands on her shoulders.

Her fingers uncurled automatically as he drew her on to her feet.

'What do you think you're doing?' she demanded. 'This is my house. You've no right——'

'And you've no right to call me a gigolo,' he rasped. 'It's a ludicrous accusation in any case, given the circumstances.'

The circumstances of his having more financial power

than most people ever dreamed of, thought Damaris, still seething. 'Don't you dare——' she began.

But her words were cut off by his lips. She felt his tongue force itself between her clenched teeth as his hands moved down her back, pressing her against him. For a moment she tried to struggle, but he only held her harder, in a grip from which she had to admit she didn't much want to escape. His mouth was harder too, his tongue exploring her mouth as if he owned it—which indeed, at this instant, he did. Now his thumb was revolving slowly at the base of her spine, causing her to gasp with a mixture of anger and—there was no denying it—desire such as she had never felt before. Soon she was responding to that need, which only made her angrier, so that her response became as avenging as his. As his lips twisted against hers she moved her head and sank her teeth awkwardly into tender flesh.

He grunted and lifted his face for a second, amber eyes blazing. Then, to her utter bewilderment, once more he covered her mouth with his.

Now Damaris tasted salt mingled with a remembered sweetness, and she pulled away to gaze with stunned disbelief at what she'd done.

A small drop of blood had formed on his lower lip and her eyes widened, but Joel only bent his head again, and this time, although his kiss started out as a reprisal, after a while it softened, becoming searching and almost gentle. His arms, no longer imprisoning, held her quite gently too, and this second, much sweeter kiss seemed to go on for an eternity that was even more intoxicating than their first fiery confrontation.

When it was over Joel stared down at her with a faintly baffled look in his eyes. 'Well, wasp,' he said softly. 'I said you wouldn't get away with it, didn't I?'

Damaris swallowed. 'Yes, you did. But I don't think you got away with much either.' She touched a finger lightly to his lip, which wasn't swollen but still showed the faint mark of her teeth.

'Maybe not.' He held her away from him. 'Apparently my wasp has a sting.'

Damaris swallowed again, and took a long, deep breath. 'I'm sorry,' she said shortly, not quite meeting his eyes.

'What for? Biting me? Or suggesting I take money for services rendered?'

'Both,' she said resolutely after a long hesitation. 'I don't know what it is about you, Joel, but you seem to have a terrible effect on my temper.'

'Your temper's not the only thing I have an effect on, is it?' he remarked, bedroom eyes glinting.

Damaris eyed him warily, and suddenly his wounded lips parted in a melting smile. 'I'm sorry too,' he admitted. 'I should have known better than to let you rile me. And I didn't have any right to take revenge.'

Damaris smiled back a little guiltily. 'No, you hadn't. But I do concede the mutual provocation.' Her smile broadened into an impish grin. 'All things considered, though, I found it rather—stimulating.'

'Did you indeed? So my wasp has a taste for blood, has she?' He raised his eyebrows derisively. 'Interesting.' When he saw the horrified expression on her face he added quickly, 'I was only teasing. Let's start this over from the beginning.'

'What do you mean?'

'Pretend I've just come in, and that I've asked you out for a meal.'

'Oh,' said Damaris. 'Well, it's very kind of you, but I haven't a sitter.'

'Get one.'

'I suppose I could, but Ginny's got a bit of a cold. She may wake up and want me. Besides—neither of us is really dressed for dinner.'

'What are you talking about?'

'Well, you're wearing an old leather jacket and I've got jeans on.'

'Take them off,' he suggested, with a predatory leer.

'Joel!' Damaris glared at him.

He held up his hands. 'Sorry. Wishful thinking. But, my dear girl, this is Vancouver. There are a million restaurants which serve perfectly good food without demanding a tie and tails.'

'I know,' said Damaris, 'but I thought——'

'You thought they were beneath my dignity.' He sighed. 'My dear, I know you find it hard to believe, but underneath this dignified exterior lurks a perfectly human male—who is beginning to feel decidedly hungry.'

'Dignified exterior indeed!' scoffed Damaris. 'All right, I take your point. All the same, I honestly don't think I ought to go out this evening.'

Irritation flared in his eyes, and vanished. 'Commendably maternal,' he murmured without enthusiasm as he turned away from her to stare disgustedly out at the garden. When he turned back, his expression had changed and he was peeling off his leather jacket. 'I have a solution,' he announced triumphantly. 'I'll cook dinner for the two of us. Right here.'

Damaris blinked. '*You'll* cook dinner,' she echoed. 'But—can you *cook?*'

'Certainly. Can you?'

'Yes, of course. But I don't get it. . .'

'What don't you get? The fact that I'm capable of

preparing my own food without the assistance of a bevy of chefs and butlers?'

'Well—yes.'

'I thought so. For your information, I don't have a butler. I do have a cook, but that doesn't mean I'm utterly helpless. The sight of a saucepan doesn't bring on a fit of the vapours, I promise you.'

Damaris giggled at the thought of Joel indulging in vapours. 'I didn't suppose it would,' she assured him. 'Gourmet cooking is a hobby of yours then, is it?'

'It is not. I don't have time for hobbies. And there's nothing gourmet about my cooking. It was a practical necessity when I was growing up. Both my parents worked, and I was the eldest of——' He hesitated. '—four children. So I was expected to get supper on after school. Believe me, there was never any question of gourmet.'

'No, I guess not.' Damaris sat down hastily, because Joel was now pushing up the sleeves of his beige pullover and she had to admit that there was nothing remotely incapable about the muscular play of his forearms either. 'Didn't you have any sisters?' she asked.

She saw his shoulders stiffen for a second before he replied lightly. 'What a very unliberated question. Don't tell me you think the job should have been relegated to girls?'

'Not at all, but I'm a realist. That's what always happened in our household.'

'Not in ours.' He paused. 'Yes, I did have a sister. She was three years younger.'

He had his back to her now, and was rummaging efficiently through her cupboards. But there was something about the set of his shoulders and the way his voice had suddenly turned brusque that made her hesitate.

'Did—did you say *was*?' she asked doubtfully. 'Isn't she——?'

'No,' said Joel, still with his back to her. 'She isn't. She died when she was fourteen. There was an operation that might have saved her, but my parents couldn't afford the fare to New York.'

'Oh,' gasped Damaris, as understanding dawned at last. 'Oh, Joel, I'm so sorry. So *that*'s why you agreed to be the mystery man. It seemed so—so out of character.' She stared at his back which had gone unnaturally rigid. 'Oh, I *am* sorry. Was she—were you very close to her?'

'Yes. She was my only sister.'

Was that a break she heard in the warm deep voice? Without thinking, Damaris got up and put her arms around his waist in a gesture that was meant to comfort, and Joel turned around and let his hands drop on to her shoulders. 'It's all right, wasp,' he said gently. 'Thanks for caring. You're really a very nice girl, aren't you?'

She looked up and saw that he was smiling, a smile that was edged with pain, and his eyes reflected the memory of an old grief that had not yet been laid to rest.

'I don't think I'm really a girl any more, Joel,' Damaris said shakily. 'As a twenty-seven year old mother of one, I don't qualify.'

'Never mind. You're still very nice.' He dropped a kiss lightly on to her forehead, and then said briskly, 'Now, where were we?'

'*You* were messing about in my cupboards. Were you looking for anything in particular?'

'Food, preferably. Just plain food.'

'Macaroni?' suggested Damaris.

'Perfect. Where is it?'

'Look, I'll fix it——'

'You will not. I intended to take you out, so the least

I can do is cook. You sit there and direct operations. I suspect you're quite good at that.'

'And what's *that* supposed to mean?' she demanded.

Joel grinned and was about to answer when there was a sudden howl from upstairs.

By the time Damaris had soothed and settled a fretful Ginny and returned to the kitchen, Joel was sliding a large casserole out of the oven.

'Macaroni cheese,' he announced, depositing it on the table. He opened the fridge. 'And green salad.'

'It looks wonderful. We can eat in the dining-room,' began Damaris.

'Nonsense. Macaroni should always be eaten in kitchens. Much cosier.'

'Cosier?' she choked, never having thought of cosiness as a word to be associated with Joel.

'More intimate,' he amended.

Yes, that was more like him. She smiled, and sat down at the kitchen table which he had already set for two.

After the first pangs of hunger had been staved, Damaris laid down her knife and fork and said tentatively, 'You must have been a very close family, you and your parents and brothers—and your sister.'

'We were. Of course I was supposed to be in charge of my brothers while my parents worked, and they resented it. So we fought a lot. Still do,' he added wryly.

'I believe you. Are they all here in Vancouver?'

'No, my parents live in the Bahamas. Better for Mother's health, which isn't too robust any more. My brothers all run enterprises back east. John's standing as a federal candidate next time round.'

'Oh, yes. I think I read something about that. Was it your idea to settle your parents in the Bahamas?'

'More or less. And they were agreeable. After

Jacqueline died I vowed no member of my family would ever again suffer from lack of money. They haven't.'

No, thought Damaris, they wouldn't. She was at last beginning to understand the powerful forces which motivated this astoundingly successful man—who could still turn his hand to macaroni when the need arose, and who, for all his success, had never felt the need to deny his roots. He wasn't really such a brute after all. Strange he had never got married. . .

She frowned, and peered doubtfully into the wine which Joel had produced from somewhere—presumably his car because she didn't think she had any in the house. Surely, ages ago, she had read something about a wedding. . .?

'What's the matter?' asked Joel. 'What have I done now? You're scowling like a witch on the warpath.'

'Mmm?' She looked up, startled. 'Oh, you haven't done anything. I just remembered, or at least I *think* I remember. . .' She stopped.

'What do you think you remember?'

'Well—no, it's none of my business.'

'That never stopped you before,' he observed drily. 'What's none of your business?'

She put down the wine glass and stared resolutely at a point just above his eyebrows. 'Joel—were you married once? I seem to remember. . .'

'Yes,' he said briefly. 'I was.'

'Oh, and——'

'And I'm not married any more. Right again.'

Damaris stopped staring at the faint lines on his forehead and forced herself to look into his eyes. They were deep, dark amber and oddly cold. Funny; she hadn't thought that amber could be cold.

'I'm sorry,' she said. 'I told you it was none of my business.'

'Oh, there's no secret. Every lurid detail was in the papers. I was married eight years ago to a girl I met on holiday while I was visiting my parents. It was a whirl-wind romance, we married in great haste, spent a year repenting at leisure—at least I did—and then spent rather longer getting divorced. Served me right. At the age of thirty, and as the head of several thriving car dealerships, I was quite old enough, and should have been wise enough, to know better.'

'Better than what?'

'Than to marry a nineteen-year-old sex-kitten with her brain located in—no, that's not true. There was nothing the matter with Sharon's brain. She knew what she wanted and she got it.'

'You sound bitter. Surely it takes two. . .and she *was* very young.'

'Yes.' His voice was clipped. 'And, as I said, I should have known better. I suppose I was ripe for the plucking by then though. Didn't have much time for serious relationships while I was getting my companies established.'

'I see. So—when it didn't work out, did you——?'

'Did I throw her out on her ear? Not exactly. She left the marriage considerably better off than she started.'

That hadn't been what Damaris was going to ask, but she seemed to have received her answer. Thirty-year-old, brilliant, successful Joel Agar had become bored with his child-bride once he'd satisfied his passion and thrown her out, not on her ear precisely, but with suitable compensation for her time.

Well, as she'd said, it was none of her business, and there was nothing written in rock that said she had to admire him. All the same, she felt a tightening somewhere deep in her chest as if a small hole had opened in her heart.

Joel was standing up now, clearing away the dishes. 'Let's not discuss my less than impressive past,' he said firmly, echoing Damaris's own thoughts. 'Let's clear up this mess and move on to more—what was that word you used?—*stimulating* pursuits.'

Damaris glared at him. 'I'll deal with the dishes. You cooked,' she said, equally firmly. 'And we're not moving on to anything.'

'Hmm.' He studied her thoughtfully, amber-brown eyes gleaming annoyingly. 'What do you find to amuse yourself with in the evenings then, my dear?'

'I garden,' she said dampeningly.

'In the winter?'

'It's not winter. And I read. I also have a child and a cat to look after, and, if you must know, I work with a couple of girls' clubs and visit at an old people's home. I'm not totally without initiative, you know.'

'I didn't suppose for a moment that you were. As I said earlier, you're a very nice—woman, Damaris Gordon. Why have you turned back into a wasp?'

He was looking at her with such teasing charm, such smiling tenderness, that Damaris couldn't stay indignant any longer.

'I haven't turned back into a wasp,' she said, helping him to stack the dishes. 'All the same, just in case you're under any misapprehensions, this evening will be strictly chaste.'

Joel heaved an exaggerated sigh. 'How dull for both of us,' he murmured. Then, as Damaris's grey eyes started to fill with smoke, he added quickly, 'I take it back. We'll spend an inspiring evening watching that gardening show on TV.'

'Great idea. I like gardening,' replied Damaris, refusing to react to his sarcasm.

'So I gathered. How would you like to come and argue with *my* gardener for me? He keeps trying to plant vegetables where I want flowers and shrubs.'

'Vegetables are good for you,' said Damaris, looking pious. 'But so are flowers,' she felt obliged to add. 'Good for the spirit, anyway.'

'Mm. Good for wasps too, I believe.'

Damaris threw a tea-towel at him, and he grabbed it and looped it round her neck, pulling her towards him till her chest was just touching his. 'You watch it, my girl,' he ordered, his lips very close to her own.

She *was* watching it, closely, but Joel only smiled and released her.

A few minutes later they were seated in front of the television, side by side at a distance carefully maintained by Damaris, who was pretending to a virtuous fascination with the care and feeding of rhododendrons.

When the programme was over, Joel laid a long arm along the back of the sofa and shifted his thighs on the cushions. Damaris eyed him warily as his fingers brushed casually against her shoulder, but he was staring straight ahead at the wall and appeared to be innocently absorbed with the progress of an ant along a knot in the light pine panelling.

'Would you like to watch something else?' she asked cautiously.

He turned his head slowly. 'No.'

'Oh.'

'I think you know what I'd like to do,' he said, his

eyes locking with hers, and his lips parted just enough to give her a glimpse of his teeth.

'Is that all you came for?' asked Damaris resentfully, not bothering to pretend she didn't know what he meant.

'I thought it was,' he replied enigmatically.

Damaris frowned. 'Well, you can think again,' she informed him.

'I know. I am.' The backs of his fingers began to caress her neck.

She started to pull away, then found that she didn't want to, and soon Joel's hand was cupping the back of her head, turning her to face him. She couldn't move; she was hypnotised by those eyes, burning into her like glowing copper. He bent towards her and her lips parted.

What might have happened next Damaris never knew, because just at that moment Candy, who seemed to have appeared out of nowhere, leaped on to her lap with an imperious little meow and began to knead sharp claws into her jeans.

Damaris jumped, and Joel swore convincingly. 'Where the hell did that beast come from?' he growled.

'She's not a beast. I expect she came down from my bed.'

'You mean to say you sleep with that furry abomination?'

'Sometimes,' replied Damaris, tight-lipped.

'She's disgustingly fat,' observed Joel morosely.

'I think she's pregnant.'

'Good heavens. Don't you know it's irresponsible to bring more unwanted animals into the world? Have you any idea how many cats the SPCA has to put down each year?'

'Don't sound so damned sanctimonious! I got her from the SPCA, and I suspect she was already pregnant.'

'I see.' Joel had the grace to look abashed. 'I suppose I was sanctimonious. And I should have known.'

'Known what?'

'That you have a kind heart and more sense than I gave you credit for.'

'Is that a compliment, Mr Agar?'

He grinned. 'Certainly not. But you can take it as an apology if you like.'

'Generous of you.'

'I know.' He fixed a bleak eye on Candy's purring black and ginger bulk. 'Can't you move it away?'

'She's not an it.'

'All right, can't you move *her* away?'

'Why?'

'Because I want to kiss you—chastely, I promise.' Joel reached across to deposit a highly disgruntled Candy on to the floor.

'But——' began Damaris.

But Joel's arms were already around her waist and he was bending her against the arm of the sofa. Once again his lips hovered close to hers.

And once again they were interrupted.

'Ma-maa,' came a childish wail from upstairs. It was followed by several loud sneezes and a cough.

Damaris pushed Joel away and leaped up, leaving him sprawled across the sofa with his eyes fixed disgustedly on the ceiling.

It was some time before she came downstairs again, after rocking Ginny into a fitful sleep, and by that time Joel was standing in the front hall putting on his jacket.

'You're leaving,' she said unnecessarily.

'Very observant of you. Yes, I fear the combined forces of your cat and your kid may drive me to do something illegal if I stay here much longer. I might get away with catricide, if there is such a thing, but I'm told the law has a most unreasonable restriction on infanticide.'

Damaris glared. She seemed to spend a lot of time glaring at Joel. 'You're not at all reasonable yourself,' she told him. 'Children need care and attention. You ought to understand that, considering you looked after your family so often when you were young.'

'Oh, I do understand it,' he assured her. 'In fact I imagine it's my early acquaintance with the responsibilities of parenthood that has left me with very little enthusiasm for anything on two legs under twelve.'

'You mean you think they *improve* after twelve?' Damaris wasn't sure that she had heard right.

'Not at all, but I found that by the time they reached that age I finally had it established who was boss. Besides, they could always be blackmailed into doing my chores for me, or persuaded to go out and play in traffic.'

'You have no scruples,' said Damaris crossly, not sure if he was teasing her nor not.

'None whatever,' he agreed cheerfully. 'Don't you like unscrupulous men, Damaris Gordon?'

His hand was on the back of her neck again, and Damaris wasn't at all sure what she liked at this moment, so she didn't answer. Joel looked down at her, laughing at her discomposure, planted a light kiss on her disapproving lips and said, 'Goodnight, wasp. See you soon.'

She was still gaping after him in wide-eyed astonishment as he clicked the door smartly shut behind him.

Damaris rubbed the back of her hand across her eyes. Surely this evening had to be some kind of waking dream—or nightmare? She had spent nearly two weeks bewildered and half bewitched by Joel's campaign of roses; and now, after the roses, had come Joel himself—

and she was more confused than ever. Not about her attraction to him: that needed no spelling out. But about how she intended to handle it.

Resting her hand on the banister, she trailed slowly up the stairs to bed.

Perhaps there wasn't any need to handle it at all, she decided after a while. Just because she didn't want to get involved with a man again—especially a man who disliked cats and children, and had cavalierly ended his marriage as soon as his young wife had ceased to amuse him—didn't mean she had any cause to worry.

Joel hadn't been in the least amused by the interruptions to his activities on this evening which hadn't gone at all as he had planned. When he left he had said, 'See you soon,' but that meant nothing. It was entirely possible he wouldn't call her again.

But in that Damaris was wrong.

He called her the very next day and suggested that, if Ginny was better, perhaps she would like to take in the play at the Queen Elizabeth Playhouse at the weekend?

Damaris opened her mouth to say, 'Thank you, but I don't think so,' and found herself saying, 'I'd love to,' instead.

CHAPTER FIVE

'SO HOW was he?' enquired Chloe the next day as she bounced into Damaris's kitchen dressed, quite conventionally for a change, in jeans and a halter-neck.

'How was who?' asked Damaris, eyeing her friend with disfavour. She hadn't yet had it out with Chloe about her perfidy over the key.

'Joel Agar, of course. The hunk.'

'I don't know. I didn't sample him.'

Chloe's eyes widened. 'You didn't? Goodness, you must have the libido of a rock to be able to resist lips like that.'

'Oh,' said Damaris carelessly, 'I didn't resist *those*.'

'Ah,' exclaimed Chloe. 'Well, that's a start. I'm surprised though; I thought he'd work faster than that.'

'I expect he does, given half a chance. Which he wasn't.' Damaris took a deep breath. 'Chloe, what in hell do you mean by giving him my key? I suppose you were all in on some plot to ruin my evening?'

'No, we weren't,' replied Chloe. 'I told you before, I think you're quite capable of managing your own life. Mary may have been plotting for all I know, but the truth is, I took one look at your Joel and decided I'd be doing you a favour. He said he wanted to surprise you, and he's exactly the sort of surprise *I'd* give my teeth for.'

'Well, I wouldn't,' snapped Damaris. Then she saw Chloe's merry eyes fastened on her with such beguiling friendliness that she found she couldn't stay angry any more. 'I doubt if you'd get him without your teeth in,' she remarked, grinning. 'Never mind, it doesn't really matter.'

'Good,' said Chloe. 'So what did the two of you do, if you didn't——?'

'He cooked,' Damaris interrupted quickly. 'He's a much better cook than I am. I could never turn macaroni into an adventure the way he did.'

Chloe extracted a squashed tofu and green cheese sandwich from her back pocket and bit into it pensively. 'Yes, that's very unpleasant, isn't it?' she murmured, turning up her nose and adopting a ladylike accent. 'We don't discuss that sort of thing, my dear. Too demoralising.'

Damaris chuckled, cast a dubious eye at her friend's questionable sandwich, and agreed that perhaps they'd better not discuss cooking. But when Chloe left a few minutes later she wished she could at least *think* about food. Instead, inevitably, her thoughts slipped into an old groove. Why was Joel, who could obviously have anyone he wanted—even Chloe—wasting his time on a woman with mousy hair and a skinny figure who assured him she didn't want him?

In the end she gave up trying to make sense of it and, despite her misgivings, began to look forward to the weekend.

As it turned out, by the time the evening actually arrived Damaris had almost convinced herself that Joel wouldn't show up after all—in spite of the fact that she was ready and waiting and wearing her favourite green dress with the flaring skirt.

But he did show up, right on time, and bearing more beautiful roses.

'Oh, Joel,' she exclaimed, a little wildly. 'They're

lovely. But. . .' She waved an arm round the living-room which was still buried under a colourful profusion of his earlier rosy excesses. 'But where am I going to put them?'

'In the kitchen,' said Joel promptly. 'In memory of our night of passion that wasn't.'

Damaris laughed. 'And we're not going to have one either,' she assured him.

'Apparently not—not in this house anyway.' He cast a baleful look at Candy, who was stalking across the floor with her tail curled over at the end.

'Well, at least we're of the same mind about that,' said Damaris.

By the end of the evening she had discovered that they were of the same mind about a lot of things. Both of them were relieved that the play was a modern comedy instead of something relevantly Canadian, and when they went for supper afterwards Damaris was delighted that the restaurant he chose featured manageable portions and good service.

That was one of the many nice things about Joel, she reflected a couple of weeks later. By then she had been out with him several times, having found it impossible to refuse his invitations, and not once had he taken her to the sort of place where bored staff regularly interrupted all conversation to chirp with insincere concern, 'Is everything all right then?' She had almost forgotten what it was like to eat in an establishment where the staff was expected to *know* that everything was all right. Chloe, with whom she most frequently ate out, favoured cheap, often mysterious food in small cafés.

Yes, being entertained by Joel was extremely pleasant. She could easily get used to it. And when he wanted to be nice he was very good at it. Almost as good as he was at being a bastard, she thought ruefully, remembering some of their earlier encounters.

She refused to allow herself to think about where all this was leading, knowing only that she was enjoying herself as she never had with Scott or Craig, and that she didn't want this interlude to end. But at the back of her mind she knew it *would* end.

Joel hadn't tried to seduce her again, contenting himself with kisses—if contenting was the right word. His kisses left Damaris hungering for much more. But in her household, with a bright and bouncy Ginny completely recovered from her cold and a cat who thought she owned her owner, there wasn't much opportunity for seduction. Besides, for some inexplicable reason Joel seemed to have become the soul of respectful propriety.

Once she had asked him how he found the time to see her so often, given his responsibilities, and he had answered rather tersely that time was his servant not his master and that that was one of the advantages of success.

One evening early in May when they were sitting in the garden arguing about the shape of a cloud, more out of habit than conviction, Joel changed the subject suddenly and asked her if she would like to visit the sea-lions.

'Sea-lions,' Damaris repeated blankly.

'At the mouth of the Fraser. They're resting there on their annual migration. Don't you ever read the papers?'

'Of course I do. But I don't see how we're going to get there without a boat.' She was indignant, wondering if Joel meant to spend the rest of the evening being as patronising as only he could be.

'I have a boat.'

Of course. He would have. 'Thank you,' she replied coolly, 'that might be nice, and I imagine Ginny——'

'No,' said Joel. 'Not Ginny. Just you.'

Damaris sighed. She might have known. Although Joel now tolerated Ginny, and treated her with a sort of distant kindness, he showed no interest in becoming closer to the little girl, and whenever she cried or whined he just raised his eyebrows and muttered something about having thought he'd got away from all that when he left home.

But when he saw that Damaris was looking mutinous, he said firmly, 'A yacht's not the place for a child, you know, my dear. At least not if I'm distracting her mother—as I intend to.'

He dropped his arms over her shoulders and pulled her against him, and Damaris, oddly short of breath, found herself giving in to his persuasion.

'All right, you win,' she conceded. 'I'll get Jane to look after Ginny. Is it a big boat?'

'Seventy feet.'

'Big enough,' she said, trying not to look too impressed. 'When shall I arrange for Jane?'

'Saturday. The sea-lions will be moving on soon.'

'That will be fine,' she agreed, and hoped she didn't sound too eager.

As it turned out, when Saturday came Damaris wasn't sure there was anything fine about it—not when she was awakened by the screaming of the alarm at an hour which she refused to believe existed.

'Horrible invention of the devil,' she muttered, as she switched off the offending timepiece. 'You're much too early.'

Then she saw the clear morning sun sparkling through

a chink in the curtains and remembered that this was the day she was to sail off into the sunrise with Joel.

It was a beautiful day, blue and bright and a little breezy, and Damaris gave a light-hearted skip as she jumped out of bed and hurried into the kitchen to start breakfast for Ginny.

When Joel arrived, dressed appropriately in white trousers and a white sweater, she gave him such a beaming smile that he blinked, almost as if he'd been dazzled by the sun.

'Good morning, wasp,' he said gruffly, his deep-set eyes glowing at her face. 'No sting today?'

'No sting,' said Damaris.

'Good.' He smiled. 'You haven't turned into a butterfly, I suppose?'

Damaris laughed. 'Wasps don't. But I could be a cabbage one if you like—seeing that I'm all dressed in white, just like you.'

'So you are. Which of us is going to make the obvious comment first?'

'You are,' said Damaris. 'I'm never obvious.'

'You can say that again,' he groaned. 'All right, let's forget about the great minds for the moment. I have something more important to discuss.'

'What——?'

But her words were cut off, as Joel took a quick stride across the kitchen, clasped her firmly in his arms, and kissed her soundly.

'That,' he replied smugly, when he had finished. 'Are you ready?'

'Ready to. . .?' She swallowed.

Joel grinned, exposing all his even white teeth. 'Ready to leave for my boat,' he explained innocently.

'Oh. Oh, yes, of course.' Damaris was flustered. 'I'll just have a word with Jane.'

'Knowing you, you've already had dozens of words with Jane,' he muttered sarcastically.

Damaris ignored him and had her discussion with the sitter—which, as Joel had correctly suggested, was the third she had had that morning.

Half an hour later the Jaguar was purring sleekly through Stanley Park to Coal Harbour.

'Oh,' said Damaris as they stood on the dock preparing to go aboard Joel's yacht. 'You called her *Jacqueline*. After your sister?'

'Yes,' he replied shortly—and, seeing his eyes darken, she said no more.

Once on board, Damaris gaped in amazement to discover that what she had been thinking of as just a large boat in fact resembled a floating condominium.

The spacious salon was panelled in oak. The small but well-stocked bar was mahogany, as were the tables, and there were two sectional sofas covered in a warm gold material that was soft and inviting to the touch. The carpet was solid tan with a black border.

'Wow,' said Damaris, throwing sophistication to the breeze. 'It's gorgeous.'

'Glad you like it,' he replied laconically. 'Would you like to see the master bedroom?'

She glanced at him doubtfully, but his face expressed only the polite concern of a host who wanted to please his guest.

'All right,' she agreed, wondering what further marvels would be revealed.

They went below and she saw that both the master bedroom and the much smaller guest bedroom were equipped with telephones and an en suite bathroom, as well as sinfully alluring beds with heavy black quilts.

She backed away hastily, to Joel's evident amusement. Once safely back in the salon, and still feeling a little stunned by this restrained display of her host's net worth, she was introduced to a tall, bearded man with dark, unhappy eyes and a cynical smile.

'This is Mike,' said Joel. 'He captains the *Jacqueline* for me.'

'That,' said Mike, the smile becoming even more cynical, 'is a polite way of saying I'm the chief cook and bottle-washer, janitor, caretaker and dogsbody extraordinaire. Occasionally I even get to sail this little tub.'

'For which you get very well-paid,' Joel reminded him mildly.

Mike shrugged. 'Of course. Why else would I be here?'

'Because you love messing about in boats, and are much too set in your ways to think of doing anything else.'

Mike gave his employer a ferocious scowl which didn't quite ring true. 'You see, Mrs Gordon? That's the appreciation I get for all my years of devotion.'

For a moment, until she caught the look of wary affection in Mike's deep eyes, Damaris half believed he was serious. Then she saw the same look reflected in Joel's eyes, and after that she was sure that here were two men who respected and understood each other well. She wondered if all Joel's employees were equally outspoken, and decided they probably weren't. If they were she suspected they didn't continue to work for him for long.

With Mike steering the *Jacqueline* effortlessly out of the harbour, Joel and Damaris sat down in the salon to consume a breakfast of waffles and bacon served by a sprite of a girl wearing shorts—and a sweater that was meant to be too tight but really wasn't, mainly because there was nothing much beneath it to conceal.

'Kirstie,' explained Joel, seeing Damaris's puzzled expression as the girl scuttled away without giving him a chance to introduce her. 'Mike's daughter.'

'Oh. I wonder why I thought he wasn't married?'

'Probably because he isn't exactly. Not any more. His wife, Ann, walked out on him three months ago. Something about there being more to life than boats, I understand.'

'You mean she walked out on her daughter too?' That Damaris was unable to conceive of any woman willingly walking out on a daughter was evidenced by the quick tightening of her mouth.

Joel shook his head. 'No, it wasn't like that at all. Mike only has her on weekends, but Kirstie loves boats so Ann's greatly outnumbered.'

'Oh, I see.' The lines around Damaris's mouth relaxed perceptibly. 'That's different.'

'Is it?'

The small smile he gave her was faintly sardonic, and she turned away from its blatant seduction to mutter belatedly, 'Poor Mike.'

'Yes.' Joel nodded. 'He's taking it hard. He used to be a happy-go-lucky individual. Nothing ever seemed to get him down. But as you must have noticed, these days he's doing his best to impersonate a dour old codger.'

'Mm,' agreed Damaris. 'His best is pretty good, isn't it? But I see now why you let him snarl at you like that. You've got a soft heart tucked away under that ruthless façade, haven't you, Mr Agar?' Her grey eyes were almost accusing, as though he had set out deliberately to mislead her.

'Certainly not,' he replied promptly. 'Whatever gave you that idea?' But the eyes that ran lazily over her now were as soft as the heart she had just accused him of hiding.

After they had finished the breakfast which Kirstie cleared hurriedly away, they sat in the salon for a while, talking desultorily, enjoying each other's company, but all the time aware of a hovering knife-edge of sensuality lurking just below the surface of their casual banter. When it became overpowering they moved out on to the deck to watch Stanley Park, the University and finally Richmond glide slowly past on the left as the breeze rocked them gently on the water.

After a while Damaris found she felt comfortable and at ease standing beside Joel at the rail—well away from the golden invitation of the sofas and the black-quilted lure of his bed. She smiled at the antics of the gulls and sandpipers, and saw no great need to keep up a conversation. Strange; she'd never thought of Joel as comfortable before. But at this moment he was making no attempt to take advantage of the fact that they were alone and unlikely to be interrupted out here on the edge of the Pacific.

Almost two and a half hours later, after they had gone inside to drink hot, aromatic coffee, talked some more, and once again wandered on to the deck, Joel announced that they were coming close to the sea-lions. Mike cut the *Jacqueline*'s engines, and Damaris leaned against the rail as Joel came up behind her to put a casual arm around her shoulder.

'Mm,' she murmured happily, taking in the frothing grey-green waters, the bright morning sky and the waves breaking against the rocks as the *Jacqueline* drew close to her destination. 'This is lovely.'

Joel, hearing the delight in her musical voice, and watching the wind whip her soft fair hair into a fluffy cloud about her face, said softly, 'Yes, isn't it?'

Without thinking, Damaris leaned her head back against his chest, and when she turned to look up at him she was startled to see a strange look in his eyes. A look that was oddly intense and yet stunned in a way, as if he'd had an unwelcome revelation.

'What is it?' she asked, suddenly anxious.

'Nothing. Look.' His arm tightened around her as he leaned across to point out the first of the sea-lions sunning itself on the rocks.

'Oh,' she exclaimed, gazing at the smooth, sea-slicked body. 'He's huge. I suppose he's the head honcho around here?'

Joel laughed. 'I don't think so. He's a California sea-lion, but most of the others are Stellers.' He waved at the group in question, about twenty or thirty of them, one or two now scuffling in the water, another sliding ponderously in behind them, and one emitting a series of not very convincing barks.

'How long will they stay?' she asked, smiling as another huge animal joined those already in the water.

'Just a few weeks. They're all males on their way to the breeding grounds, and they're here to stuff themselves on oolichans—in preparation for the serious business ahead.' He stroked a wisp of hair back behind her ear for no particular reason, and added pensively, 'I fear the human male operates rather differently. Too much gluttony tends to take his mind off reproduction.'

'Reproduction, my eye,' scoffed Damaris. 'Show me a

human male who's thinking of reproduction while he's. . .' She stopped abruptly.

'Go on,' said Joel. 'You were saying?'

'Oh, never mind,' she snapped.

'No need to take out your verbal inadequacies on me, my girl,' he reproved her. 'I thought we were going to enjoy ourselves today.'

Damaris stared up at him, wide grey eyes doubtful. 'I didn't mean to snap,' she apologised. 'It's just that. . .'

'I know, you already told me. I have a terrible effect on your temper.' He bent down suddenly and kissed her nose. 'But now let's have no more of it. Relax. Take a leaf from those characters sunning themselves over there.'

He was right, of course, and Damaris did her best to follow his good advice. But it wasn't easy. Somehow, once again, he was unnerving to be with, and although he was polite and attentive to her as they admired the sea-lions, and continued to be polite and attentive after Mike turned the *Jacqueline* around to head for home, there was a tension between them now, and she didn't know quite what to do about it. It wasn't unpleasant exactly, just distracting and a little frightening, as if something was about to happen that might turn out to be wonderful, but might just as easily be unspeakable and sad.

The breeze was stronger now and they returned to the protection of the salon. Damaris spread herself on one gold sofa section, trying to take up as much of it as she could. Joel took the hint and sat down across from her, looking amused and irritatingly confident as he took in her rigidly defensive posture.

'Don't worry,' he said drily. 'I won't have time to

assault you. Kirstie will be in with lunch in just a minute.'

'I wasn't worrying,' she retorted automatically, and then wished she'd kept quiet, because it was obvious he didn't believe her.

By the time they returned to the dock, after a salad and sandwich lunch which was rudely silent on Damaris's part, and blandly conversational on Joel's, the air between them was so electric and highly charged that Damaris, sensing Joel's growing exasperation, half expected to be taken home at once.

The end of a perfect day, she thought glumly—and then was obliged to admit that it *had* been perfect for a while. . .until she had become unaccountably bad-tempered over nothing.

'Hey! Where are we going?' she cried a few minutes later, as it dawned on her that they weren't heading anywhere near the Lions Gate Bridge and her home.

Joel took his hand off the wheel to glance fleetingly at his watch. 'Home,' he said, 'just in time for a shower, and then we'll have drinks before dinner.'

'Wh-what?' stuttered Damaris. 'But—this isn't the way to my house.'

'No,' he agreed. 'It's the way to my house. You haven't been there yet, have you?'

He knew perfectly well she hadn't been there. 'But. . .' she began. 'Joel, I can't. I have to get back to Ginny.'

'No, you don't.'

'Joel, I do. I told Jane I'd be back by five.'

'Well, you won't be, will you?'

'Joel, you can't do that. Jane may have plans.'

'She hasn't.'

'How can you possibly know that?'

'Because,' he said patiently, spinning the wheel expertly with one hand, 'as you may have noticed, there are several telephones on the *Jacqueline*. In anticipation of your objections, I took the precaution of giving young Jane a call.'

'Well, of all the high-handed, inconsiderate——'

'Nonsense. I've been very considerate. Now stop all this wailing and gnashing of teeth and prepare to enjoy the evening.'

'I am *not* wailing,' spat Damaris.

'Maybe not, but you're certainly gnashing your teeth.' He extended an arm without taking his eyes from the road, and placed a hand gently over her mouth. 'You see?'

It was true. Her lips were pressed together, and her teeth were clenched.

She pushed his hand away quickly before the urge to bite it became too strong.

'Thought better of it, did you?' he asked conversationally.

'Better of what?'

'Biting the hand that is about to feed you.'

She raised her chin and didn't answer. Did he *have* to know what she was thinking?

But it would hardly have taken a clairvoyant to divine her thoughts when, a short time later, the Jaguar turned into a tree-lined private road off Marine Drive. It was the sort of driveway that could quite well have sported lions at the entrance without looking as if its owner harboured delusions of suburban grandeur. Not that Joel had opted for lions. Only solid brick walls and a wrought-iron gate that looked as if it meant business.

As the car pulled to a stop in front of a three-storey mansion in ivy-covered red brick, Damaris let out a gasp of appreciation. She had thought her own house was luxurious when Scott had brought her there, but it couldn't hold a candle to this.

'Oh!' she exclaimed. 'Oh, Joel, what a *beautiful* old house. Is it *yours?*'

He laughed, the note of impatience which had been so noticeable earlier no longer apparent. 'I certainly hope so. I've been living in it for seven years. But it's not really old, you know. Turn of the century, I believe.'

'That's old for here,' said Damaris who, unlike Joel, had never had the chance to travel.

'True,' he agreed. 'Coming in?' His eyes, as he held out his hand to her, were smiling and gently amused.

So eyes, even ones that weren't Irish, really could smile, she thought bemusedly, taking the proffered hand and walking with him towards the big front doors.

In the spacious, oak-panelled hallway they were greeted by a sour-faced woman with small dark eyes and a nose that look more like a beak.

'This is Mrs Pritchard, Damaris,' Joel introduced her. 'My housekeeper, the boss-lady who keeps me and my house in order—and without whom I'd never find clean socks.'

'Huh,' grunted Mrs Pritchard. 'No one keeps this man in order, miss, as you've probably found out for yourself.' But the smile she gave Joel completely changed her homely countenance, belying the gruffly spoken words.

Obviously, thought Damaris, the housekeeper was another of Joel's conquests, and that dour expression most likely hid a heart of pure putty in his expert hands.

'Yes,' she agreed, grinning. 'I had noticed. Mr Agar has a habit of running things to suit himself, hasn't he? In other words, of getting his own way.'

'Not always,' he murmured, putting his hand in the small of her back and ushering her into the sitting-room. When she glanced up at him curiously there was a faintly mocking light in his eye.

'Right,' he said. 'Before we get down to business, would you like a bath, to relax your charming body after all that bracing sea air?'

'I am relaxed,' she replied crisply. 'And my body isn't charming, it's skinny.'

'Svelte,' he corrected her, with an amusement he made no attempt to hide.

Damaris, feeling a blush coming on, said quickly, 'Oh, all right, I do feel a little—well, salty. Only as I didn't know I was coming here, I don't have any clothes to change into.'

'You don't need to change,' he assured her, 'but you can borrow one of my shirts if you like. Or maybe Mrs Pritchard——'

'It's all right,' said Damaris hastily. 'I'll stay as I am.'

Joel's lips quirked. 'I thought you might. Come on, then.'

He took her arm and led her up a wide curving staircase to the next floor, along a passageway covered in thick crimson carpeting, and into a bright, blue-flowered bedroom with a sweeping view of well-kept lawns and gardens.

'The bathroom is that way,' he said, indicating a white door next to the window. 'I think you'll find everything you need—except me. But that could be re-programmed.'

'Out,' said Damaris. 'I'll manage very nicely, thank you.'

'I was afraid you would,' Joel sighed, and then beat a hasty retreat from the room as Damaris looked round for a suitable object to throw at him. Her last glimpse of him was of a white-toothed, sexy grin as he stuck his head back round the door and said, 'See you downstairs.'

'Impossible man,' she muttered as she wandered into the bathroom. All the same, she was grinning to herself when she sank down into the warm, soapy water and gazed lazily round at the gold fixtures set in marble.

Half an hour later, all bathed and scented and feeling just a little sleepy, she made her way back to the sitting-room. Joel wasn't there, so she picked up a magazine from an antique end-table and began to flip idly through the pages. Finding that the latest stock market scandal didn't interest her much, she put it down again, and just then Joel strode into the room.

'Sorry to keep you waiting,' he said. 'Had to make a couple of phone calls that wouldn't keep.'

Damaris gulped. He was wearing light grey trousers now, and was just snapping his belt into place. On top he wore nothing but a towel which was thrown carelessly around his neck, and she could still see the moisture beading on his dark bronze skin. 'Phone calls?' she croaked. 'What kind of phone calls? Joel, you haven't been organising my life again, have you? Telling Jane to stay the night or something?'

'No,' he smiled, a soft, curling smile that made an even more curdled mess of her susceptible stomach. 'Would you like me to?'

'No!' Damaris's yelp coincided with the arrival of Mrs Pritchard, who gave Joel a disapproving glare and demanded to know when he'd like dinner served, because Charlie was becoming very temperamental in the kitchen.

'Tell Charlie to have his temperament on his own time,' said Joel shortly. 'We'll eat at eight.'

'Who's Charlie?' asked Damaris, glad of the change of subject, as Mrs Pritchard, still frowning, marched off to deliver Joel's message.

'My cook. He's very good, but every now and then he gets the idea that I'm here for his convenience, rather than the other way around.'

Damaris, still disconcerted by their earlier exchange, and knowing she was being unfair, asked a little sharply, 'Are you ever anywhere for anybody's convenience but your own?'

'No, sweet wasp, not if I can help it. Although I have complete confidence you'll see to it that I never get the chance to become complacent. Can I get you a drink?'

'Yes, please,' she replied stiffly. 'It might come in handy.'

'Handy?'

'To throw at you.'

'Ah, I see. Are you about to throw a tantrum, Mrs Gordon? Because I warn you, I shan't permit it.'

'*You* won't. . .' Damaris glowered. 'And just how do you think you'd stop me?'

'Why don't you try it and find out?' He was smiling, but there was something very steely about his eyes, and Damaris decided she had no desire whatever to find out.

'Oh, just get me a drink,' she said wearily.

'I will if you ask me nicely. Vinegar, I presume?'

'Sherry, *please*,' said Damaris, with exaggerated sweetness.

'Coming up.' He went over to a small, curved bar in the corner, filled her glass and came back to present it to her with a smile that was disturbingly seductive.

'To your smoking grey eyes,' he said as he sat down opposite her, after pouring a drink for himself.

Damaris stared as he leaned back, put his arms behind

his head, and rested an ankle casually across one knee. Then her eyes rose unwittingly to the taut bare skin of his arms and chest.

'To you,' she said, a little too quickly. 'Um—thank you for today, Joel, and. . .and aren't you going to put a shirt on?'

'Do you want me to?'

'Yes,' said Damaris, with a firmness born of desperation.

'Your wish is my command. For you I'll make myself respectable—for the moment.'

He got up, eyes sparking wickedly, leaving Damaris to stare after him with a mixture of amusement, frustration and—oh, yes, damn him—more than a little desire.

When he came back he was attired in a soft white shirt which, to her consternation, made him look even more delectable than before.

'Better?' he asked. 'More suited to the occasion?'

She nodded dumbly.

'Good. Can I pour you another sherry?'

She shook her head.

'Cat got your tongue?'

She made a great effort and managed to reply lightly, 'No, of course not. I—I love this room, Joel. It's so bright and airy, and at the same time sort of mellow and old.'

'Yes. The antiques were Sharon's idea, but in the end she never actually lived here.'

'Oh, how sad,' exclaimed Damaris, trying unsuccessfully to repress an odd feeling of relief that Joel's wife had never lived in this lovely house. Then she wondered why it mattered, as Joel growled something about it not being sad in the least, and Mrs Pritchard arrived to announce that dinner was served.

Joel glanced at the clock on the mantel. 'Ten to eight,' he observed. 'Round two to Charlie.'

He swung himself on to his feet and held out a hand to Damaris.

'So you *don't* always get your own way.' She smiled as she followed him into the big, high-ceilinged dining-room. 'Charlie must be quite a free spirit. Will I meet him?'

'Not if he can avoid it. He prefers food to people, but he will accept compliments on his cooking if they're passed to him discreetly through Mrs Pritchard.'

Damaris laughed, thought of asking what would happen if one sent a disparaging message, then decided the question was redundant. If Charlie was employed by Joel, his cooking was bound to be perfect.

It was. By the end of the meal she still wasn't sure what she had eaten, but she knew it involved chicken and oranges and tasted unlike anything she'd ever sampled before. It was followed by a lemon pie that was also a delight to the taste buds. She and Joel between them consumed a bottle of expensively dry white wine, and by the time the meal was over she was feeling replete, contented and just a little giddy. She wasn't sure if the giddiness was caused by the wine or Joel's seductive and attentive presence as he sat close to her at the bottom of the long table, while Mrs Pritchard served their food with quiet efficiency.

'She's a gem,' said Damaris when they had returned to the sitting-room for coffee. 'How did you find her?'

'I learned the hard way how to see past a pretty face,' he replied wryly. 'My secretary narrowed the applicants down to three, and I chose Mrs Pritchard over a woman who insisted on regaling me with all the titles she'd worked for, and a young lady who had all the right credentials, but kept telling me *her* rules of employment. Mrs P took one look at the house and told me I ought to be ashamed of myself. So I hired her.'

Damaris laughed. 'Sometimes you surprise me, Mr Agar.'

'You surprise me all the time, Mrs Gordon.'

'You know, I don't really feel like Mrs Gordon any more,' she murmured dreamily.

Joel's eyes narrowed. 'Don't you? Who do you feel like then?'

'Oh, just Damaris, I guess.'

'Glamorous Damaris,' he drawled softly, moving to sit next to her on the sofa without troubling to ask if she minded. 'Is that what they started calling you when you changed your name?'

'No,' she replied, 'of course not. There was never any danger of that.'

'Don't underestimate yourself, sweetheart.'

'I'm not your sweetheart,' she said, edging away from him.

Joel's lips curved obliquely. 'How true. But that can always be remedied.'

'Joel!' She blinked at him, her heart thumping crazily in her chest. 'Joel, don't.'

'Don't what?'

'Don't—don't tease me about my looks.'

'I'm not teasing you.'

His eyes were that deep copper colour again, and as Damaris gazed at him anxiously, feeling a bit like a rabbit being lined up for supper by a snake, he leaned forward suddenly and cupped her face in his hands.

'You've very lovely, you know,' he said quietly. 'You

have the sweetest face and the deepest, most seductively beautiful voice of any woman I've known. Why are you afraid to accept compliments?'

'I'm not afraid. At least. . .'

'Yes, you are. Are you afraid of me?'

She couldn't look at him. 'Yes,' she whispered, her eyes on the muscles of his neck.

He slipped a hand beneath her chin and tilted her face up. 'Don't be. I want to make love to you. Not hurt you. Don't you know that?'

Yes, perhaps she knew that, but it didn't mean he *wouldn't* hurt her. 'I. . .' she began, opening her mouth and searching for words to explain. 'I. . .' she tried again.

'You,' said Joel firmly, 'are very much in need of being kissed.'

Suiting action to words, he tangled one large hand in the soft hair at her neck and pulled her head towards him. At the same time he wrapped his free arm around her waist, so that she found herself trapped against his chest with her legs pressed hard against his thighs. Then his mouth had covered hers, very slowly and completely, and all the remembered sweetness came flooding back. Her hands moved up to grasp his shoulders, then they were sliding beneath his shirt to explore his back, his chest, and every part of him that her hungrily seeking fingers could caress.

Now Joel was unfastening the buttons of her white blouse, flicking open her bra with an expertise which, just for a moment, gave her pause. But after that all she could think of was the feel of his lips as they moved down to cover her body with kisses, and his hands as they touched her breasts almost reverently and then moved to her shoulders to ease her against the cushions.

Without knowing quite how it happened, she found herself lying on the sofa with Joel's hard body half on top of her. She could feel the muscles of his leg along her thighs. . .

And it wasn't enough. She wanted to make love to Joel, desperately and with a need she hadn't known was in her. But somehow, in spite of the tumultuous urgings of her body, she knew she needed more than just a quick and violent release from the hunger that was consuming them both. Some small part of her brain was still functioning as it always had, and now this small part made her cry out as Joel's fingers began to slide inside her waistband. 'Joel! Joel, no!'

For a second he paid no attention, his hand continuing its sweet assault on her senses. Then, as her words began to penetrate, he stopped. His body still covered hers, and she could feel his muscles cord like twisted rope against her skin.

He lifted his head to stare down at her, his eyes very bright and not quite believing. 'What is it?' he asked, his voice all soft with passion. 'What's the matter, sweetheart?'

'I—Joel, please don't. I can't. . .'

'Damaris.' Her name was almost a groan. 'Damaris, I want you. You want me. Why. . .?'

'I can't,' she cried, suddenly panic-stricken. 'I just can't, that's all.' Frantically she began to claw at his shoulders, trying to push him away.

Joel swore, glaring into her eyes with a look of such pain and frustration that she was almost moved to give in. Then he pulled himself abruptly away.

As she watched him, her grey eyes clouded with misery, he turned his back on her, walked over to the window and leaned on the sill with both hands.

For several seconds there was silence, until Damaris whispered brokenly, 'I'm sorry.'

'Yes,' he said, not turning round. 'You should be.'

'Joel. . .?'

He swung to face her then, his eyes no longer copper, but flat and brown. 'Damaris, I won't pretend to understand, but let me assure you I'm not in the habit of making love to women against their will. Nor am I used to being played with. At least not recently.'

'I wasn't playing with you. I *do* want you, but. . .'

'But what? Are you holding out for marriage?' His eyes weren't flat any more. They were dark with suspicion.

'No!' cried Damaris. 'Marriage is the last thing I want.'

'I see.' A look that was partly relief and partly exasperated confusion flicked briefly across his face. 'I'm also beginning to see why old Scott did himself in on that rock-face.'

Damaris closed her eyes. 'He didn't do himself in. He fell. It was an accident. And it happened because he wouldn't accept that he wasn't a young buck any more. He insisted on trying a climb he wasn't up to.'

'Perhaps he felt he had to convince his young wife he was still a man. I can appreciate his problem.'

Damaris gasped and turned her face into the cushions without answering.

A moment later she felt his hand on her shoulder. 'I'm sorry, wasp. That was inexcusable. And I do know better.'

She gulped, sniffed, and pushed herself into a sitting position. 'It's all right. I understand. You were angry and frustrated.'

'Among other things,' he agreed drily, bending down

to pull her blouse around her shoulders. 'Not that that's any excuse.' As she gaped up at him, he began to fasten her buttons with firm, deft fingers.

'Listen,' he said, straightening as soon as he'd finished, 'I was going to tell you. I have to go away on Monday. I have business in Japan and Hong Kong, but I should be back in a week or two. I'll take you home now, and that'll give us both time to think things over. We can straighten out this mess when I get home.'

Her eyes followed him as he walked away from her to lean against the window, facing her this time, with his arms folded on his chest and his long legs crossed at the ankles. She took in the short, burnished brown hair, the heavy-lidded, amber-brown eyes—and those lips that had acted as a magnet from the first moment she had seen him standing proud and arrogant above the crowd of eager women beneath him.

She looked for a long time, and Joel returned her look, smiling a little wearily. Then she said coldly and very clearly, 'I appreciate the thought, Joel. And yes, I'd like you to take me home please. But I—I don't think we'd better see each other again. If you're leaving anyway, this is obviously the time to say goodbye.'

CHAPTER SIX

THE weary smile was wiped instantly from Joel's face, but the look he gave her now was not hurt or angry. It was hard, searching. 'Why, Damaris?' he asked harshly. 'Because I want to make love to you? Or is it because of what I said about your husband?' His lip curled in a sneer that seemed to be directed more at himself than at her. 'I've apologised for that once, and I've already told you I know it isn't true. To be honest, I can't imagine that any man married to you would be fool enough to risk his life deliberately.'

Damaris didn't want to know what he meant by that, so she didn't ask. 'It's not because of what you said,' she told him hopelessly. 'Or because you want to make love to me.'

'Then *why?*'

'Joel, I can't answer that. I just know I can't go on seeing you.' She raised her eyes, and noted that he suddenly looked haggard, older. 'Why does it matter so much?' she asked, puzzled. 'I mean—surely you only started taking me out because I provided you with more of a challenge than your usual line in ladies. I admit that we seem to enjoy each other's company. . .' she smiled wanly. . .'some of the time, at any rate. But you'll survive with one less conquest to notch up on your belt. Just let me go, Joel. Leave me in peace. Please.'

He turned away from her, his body stiffening, and as she watched, open-mouthed, he slammed his fist against

105

the wall so hard that a group of china shepherds rattled drunkenly and almost fell off their shelf.

'Oh, I'll survive,' he said bitterly, still with his back to her. 'Although, believe it or not, I don't have a "usual line" in ladies. As to why it matters—I'm damned if I know.'

Abruptly he swung round, crossed the room, and bent down to pull her to her feet. 'All right. Have it your own way,' he grated. 'Let's get moving.'

Dumb with misery, Damaris followed him as he strode ahead of her through the door. She wanted to call out to him to stop, to tell him she didn't mean it. But something stopped her. Although she hadn't yet had a chance to sort out her feelings, that part of her mind that wasn't totally absorbed by Joel still kept her from acting on a wild impulse to run after him, fling her arms around his waist and beg him not to listen to a word she'd said.

Only twenty minutes later the Jaguar slammed to a halt in front of her house, after a ride through the streets of Vancouver that would have had the Traffic Squad on its ears if they'd happened to be in the right place at the time.

Damaris turned to look at him then, saw his large hands clenched on the wheel and his jaw as rigid and uncompromising as rock. 'I'm sorry, Joel,' she said miserably. 'It's been a lovely day. Thank you for it—and for everything.'

Not a muscle in his face moved as he swung himself out of the car to open her door.

'Goodbye,' she whispered, stumbling to her feet beside him. She held out her hand.

His blank gaze flicked from her outstretched hand to her face and rested there with gaunt inscrutability.

'Goodbye, Damaris,' he said harshly. 'It's been—interesting.'

He didn't take the hand that was still outstretched towards him, and an instant later he climbed back into the car and drove away.

Damaris reached out automatically to pull Ginny away from the wood basket, but her eyes didn't move from the curtains which were blowing gently in the wind from the window. She was mesmerised by the movement as, in her mind, she turned over and over the events of the day before. It was a groove she hadn't been able to get out of from the moment she had seen Joel's car pull quietly away from the kerb.

She knew now what had happened to her. Somewhere in the course of the past few exhilarating weeks she had fallen in love with Joel Agar. It was what she had been afraid of, without wanting to admit it, from the very first time she had seen him. That had been more than half the reason for her initial antagonism—the antagonism that had made him name her 'wasp'. And her fear had not been unfounded.

Since Scott had died so suddenly, trying to prove he was still a young man instead of a middle-aged executive of forty-six, Damaris had taken great care to avoid situations which might put her in a position to meet men. Not because she couldn't handle them, or thought they'd be flocking to her door, but because she was aware that beneath her need for security and independence lay another, perhaps even deeper hunger. A hunger for love. Now she had found her love and, just as she had feared, that love had become an overwhelming threat.

A gust of wind, stronger than the others, blew the

curtain right inside the room, and Damaris got up to close the window.

Why? she thought, gazing at the bright orange tulips beside the door. Why had she let herself fall in love with Joel? He was like some magnetic star, drawing everything around him into his orbit. Including her. But the only orbit she wanted to be in was her own. She had been contented and secure here with Ginny. Not bored. Just contented.

But she wasn't contented any more.

'All right, Damaris,' she said out loud, causing Ginny to giggle. 'All right. So you're in love. And he doesn't love you. That was what made you run away last night. Wasn't it?'

No, she answered herself silently. That wasn't it. Joel might not be in love with her but he certainly wanted her, even seemed to care about her sometimes. Given time, it was possible he might come to feel more. . .

She tugged moodily at a button on her shirt. Yes, but where would that leave her? It would leave her in love with, maybe even married to, a man who wouldn't accept Ginny. The fact that he didn't like Candy could be worked out, but she couldn't allow a man who didn't love her child to become the focal point of her life.

Oh, she had made the right decision all right. Even if it broke her heart she was better off ending the relationship now—before it was too late. Before she became so inextricably linked with Joel that she would never be able to escape him.

She pulled Ginny out of the wood basket for the second time, refusing even to consider the unbearable notion that perhaps it was already too late.

A plane roared overhead, breaking her train of

thought, and Damaris collected her daughter and moved slowly into the kitchen to start supper.

'Guess what?' said Chloe, arriving unexpectedly in Mary's living-room as Damaris sat with her neighbour drinking coffee.

'What?' responded Mary and Damaris in chorus.

'Sebastian and I are leaving for Paris tomorrow.'

'Sebastian?' queried Mary, raising an eyebrow.

'The new man in my life. He's a sculptor from Seattle. He's not as gorgeous as your Joel, Damson, but he has a *mind*.'

'I should hope so,' said Mary, looking down her nose. 'Mr Agar also has a *brain*.'

Damaris stared into her coffee and said nothing.

Chloe darted a shrewd look at her friend and said, 'Hah. Trouble in Paradise, I see.'

'No trouble,' replied Damaris quietly. 'It's over. I stopped seeing Joel a week ago.'

'Yes, and I've just been telling her she's a fool,' grumbled Mary.

Chloe shrugged. 'Probably, but that's her business.'

'And what's more,' Mary continued, ignoring her, 'do you realise, Damaris, that if Chloe's leaving tomorrow you'll be quite alone?'

'Alone? What do you mean?'

'I'm off to Ottawa tomorrow. I have to see some tiresome little man about government funding. Then I'm planning a long trip down to the States.'

'That's all right,' said Damaris. 'I'll have Ginny to keep me company. And I do have friends, you know, although I'm afraid I lost track of most of them when I married Scott. He seemed to resent them.'

'Hm,' sniffed Mary. 'Another very tiresome man, your

husband. All the same, I'd feel much happier with Mr Agar on hand to keep an eye on you.'

'He's in Hong Kong,' said Damaris, attempting to close the subject.

'Yes, but he'll be back.'

'Leave her alone, Mary,' advised Chloe. 'She won't listen. And she won't fall apart if she doesn't have us around to pester her for a while.'

'No.' Damaris smiled. It was a sad, desolate sort of smile. 'I won't fall apart. But I'll miss you.'

She would too, she reflected the following day after the pair of them had left for the airport. Their company couldn't do much to cheer her, but at least when they were about she was forced to act like a human being sometimes, instead of like a despondent lump of the tofu that Chloe was always eating. She knew that her decision not to see Joel again was the right one, but being right didn't help at all. She missed him, she wanted him back, and no amount of forced gaiety put on for Ginny's sake could alter the fact that she, who had always, in a sense, been alone, was now more alone than ever.

She glared morosely at a bird chirping in a tree outside the window. Then she jumped, as Ginny, who had been playing happily with the contents of the waste-paper basket, suddenly started to cry.

Damaris checked quickly to see if the little girl had cut herself on something, but found only old bills and the usual piles of unsolicited mail.

'It's all right, Ginny,' she soothed. 'You're OK, baby.'

But Ginny wasn't OK, and a couple of hours later Damaris had to put her to bed because she'd developed a mild fever.

The next day it was worse, and she called the doctor.

'Flu,' he pronounced. 'There's a particularly nasty

summer strain going around. Just keep her cool, plenty of fluids. . .' He recited the standard litany of flu palliatives and left her with a prescription for some dubious pink liquid in a large bottle.

The doctor's advice proved correct.

Three days later Ginny was recovering nicely. Damaris, on the other hand, was not. She had had very little sleep during her daughter's illness and she hadn't been eating. Now that Ginny was better she was beginning to feel like lukewarm death herself.

The following day she felt worse, but she managed to stagger up to care for Ginny. She thought of calling the doctor again, but decided against it. He would only tell her to stay in bed, which she couldn't do unless she got someone in to care for her child. And there was no need for that. She'd be better soon.

In fact, two days later she was even worse. Ginny, completely well now, was toddling around the house again getting into things and demanding her mother's constant attention. She couldn't understand why 'Mama', who was usually so tolerant, had no patience at all when she climbed up on to the kitchen counter and began to mix powdered custard in the sink.

That night Damaris put Ginny to bed as early as she could, and then collapsed on to her own bed to fall into a restless sleep. She felt so hot and wretched that she didn't even think of Joel before her eyes closed. It was the first night she hadn't thought of him since they'd parted.

In the morning she couldn't get up.

She was awakened by a clap of thunder so loud that it rattled the windows. Then she felt Candy's claws dig hard into the blanket, and at the same moment Ginny let out a wail of fright.

'I'm coming,' muttered Damaris, attempting to put her feet on the floor. But she couldn't. Her legs wouldn't move.

She looked anxiously at the watch she'd neglected to take off the night before. It wasn't morning after all; it was early afternoon and Ginny must have been awake and hungry for hours. As well as wet.

She tried again, but it was no good.

'It's all right, Ginny,' she called weakly as another thunderclap shook the house to its foundations. 'Mama's coming.'

A streak of lightning slashed across the leaden sky and there was a strange exploding sound somewhere not far away.

'You've *got* to move,' Damaris urged herself. 'You've just got to.'

She made another stupendous effort, and this time her feet hit the floor. They didn't feel as if they belonged to her, but at least now she knew where they were.

Ginny wailed again and Damaris's eyes fell on the phone beside the bed. Help. She must have help. Mary and Chloe were gone, but she could always get Jane Spencer's mother. Shakily she reached for the receiver and held it against her ear.

The line was dead.

Now she knew what that exploding sound had been. Obviously her telephone line was down. She groaned, her head feeling as if it too were about to explode. The rest of her body felt like liquid jelly.

She made a final superhuman effort, grasped the bedpost and hauled herself on to her feet. She couldn't phone. Help was too far away. But she must reach Ginny.

Holding on to the wall, she edged her way along, and

somehow managed to stay upright until she reached the door. She stood in the opening for a moment, breathing deeply, then because there was nothing to hold on to she staggered across the hall to Ginny's room.

The little girl was sitting in her cot surrounded by stuffed animals. Her big blue eyes were wide and frightened.

Thank heavens she didn't try to climb out, thought Damaris, who knew better than anyone what her daughter was capable of.

As soon as Ginny saw her mother the fear left her eyes. There was another clap of thunder, more distant now, but this time the little blonde only laughed.

Her delighted, childish laughter was the last sound Damaris heard before a thousand coloured lights lit up the darkness in her head and she crashed down on to the daisy-patterned carpet.

The sun was beating against her eyelids, hurting, hot. Damaris put up her hand to shut it out, but she was so weak it fell back against the covers. Obstinately, she forced her eyes to open—and it wasn't the sunlight that had woken her but her own pink-shaded bedside lamp.

She frowned, and her head hurt even more. What had happened? She was at home in her own bed, but the last thing she remembered. . .

Oh, no! Ginny!

'Ginny!' She tried to scream, but all that came out was a strangled croak.

It brought results though, because immediately a man's figure appeared in the doorway. Damaris blinked. She was ill, she knew that, and the figure was sort of fuzzy, but on top of that she appeared to be suffering from major hallucinations.

She opened her eyes very wide to dispel the illusion, but that didn't help at all because now the figure was moving across the room towards her. What was more, he seemed to be glaring at her.

No illusion then. That glare was much too familiar.

'Joel,' she whispered through painfully cracked lips.

'Yes, it's me. What the hell do you mean by getting yourself in a mess like this?' His voice was gruff, angry even, but beneath the gruffness she heard unmistakable and heartfelt relief.

'Didn't mean to,' she murmured. 'Didn't realise. . .thought I could cope.'

'Idiot. Do you have to be so damned independent?'

'Not. . .independent.' Her eyes began to droop closed. 'Would have got help. The phone was down.' Her lids flew open again. 'Ginny,' she croaked, 'Joel. . .'

'Ginny's just fine. The doctor's had a look at both of you, and there's a nurse on her way over right now.'

'Nurse? I don't need. . .'

'Yes, you do. I have business to attend to or I'd damn well take you over myself. Now, stop arguing with me, woman, and go back to sleep. The doctor said that's the best thing for you.'

'But. . .'

'No buts. You frightened the hell out me, wasp, and I've had all the scares I need for one day.'

'Ginny. . .'

'The nurse will look after her too.'

Damaris nodded, too weak and weary to stand up to him. 'Yes,' she acquiesced. 'Yes. Thank you. I—thank you for coming. Goodbye, Joel.'

'Oh, no, you don't,' he replied with a fierceness that, even in her weakened state, surprised her. Without asking permission, he lowered himself on to the bed and smoothed a hand across her damp forehead. 'There'll be no more of that nonsense, young lady. You can't even be trusted to look after yourself, let alone that enterprising sprite who is currently making hay with my briefcase. You're not getting rid of me that easily. Not again.'

'Oh,' said Damaris. She heard the rough tenderness in his voice, saw concerned amber eyes with thin lines of worry around them, and as she began to drift off she mumbled drowsily, 'Bossy brute.'

But truth to tell, just at that moment, as sleep overcame her, she couldn't remember why she had wanted to get rid of him in the first place. If indeed she had.

Joel stood up and stared down at her. His hands were deep in his pockets and he was wearing a smile that was as implacable as it was tender.

'Damned right I'm bossy,' he growled. 'It's a good thing for you I am.'

But Damaris was asleep and didn't hear him.

The next time she awoke fully, there really was sun streaming through the window and a red-haired nurse was busily drawing back the curtains.

'Oh, you're awake then,' she said unnecessarily when she saw Damaris looking at her. 'And how are we today?'

'We're awful,' said Damaris, who now felt sufficiently human to realise that life could be better. 'What time is it?'

'Ten o'clock.'

She digested this. 'Um—what *day* is it?' she asked uneasily.

'Saturday. You've slept away the better part of three days.'

'Oh.' She frowned, and this time it didn't hurt as

much. Then her eyes fell on a huge bouquet of roses on the dresser. 'Joel—Mr Agar. . .?'

'He's been here every morning and evening, and on the phone every other time of day—telling me how to do my job, what to do for you, and generally getting in my way. The only thing he's been good for is keeping young Ginny entertained.'

'Joel? Ginny?' Damaris shook her head against the pillow. This was all getting too much for her—except the part about Joel telling the nurse what to do. That made sense. She smiled wryly.

A door slammed downstairs and a moment later Joel strode into the room.

'*Mr* Agar,' began the nurse, 'do you realise. . .?'

But he had eyes only for Damaris. 'You're awake,' he pronounced with satisfaction.

'I know. Nurse already told me.'

His lips twitched. 'Awake and with your tongue in good working order,' he amended. 'Thank goodness for that.'

'Mr Agar,' persisted the nurse, 'Mrs Gordon has only just woken up, she's still weak, and she hasn't had anything to eat——'

'Then get her some breakfast, Nurse Johnston.'

Damaris saw Nurse Johnston roll her eyes despairingly up at the ceiling. 'I think,' she murmured, trying not to laugh because she was afraid it might upset her insides, 'that Nurse wants you to go away for a while, Joel.'

'I don't care what Nurse wants,' he said flatly. 'I'm staying right here.'

'No, you're not. Some things are private. You can come back in fifteen minutes.'

Joel glowered, baffled and mutinous. Then, as understanding dawned at last, he turned his head away, looking gratifyingly embarrassed.

'Hm. All right, fifteen minutes,' he agreed. 'I'll go and look in on Ginny.'

'Where *is* Ginny?' asked Damaris, after he'd gone, and as Nurse Johnston began to help her with the things that were private.

'Playing in her room. You've done a good job of child-proofing it, Mrs Gordon.'

'Yes, as much as anyone can proof anything against Ginny,' her patient agreed ruefully.

'She's a going concern, I'll give you that. But she always behaves beautifully with Mr Agar. It's the only reason I put up with him.' She smiled, and Damaris knew that in spite of her words Nurse Johnston held Joel in some esteem.

'Does she really?' said Damaris, surprised. And then, suddenly anxious, 'Is she frightened of him?'

'Frightened of him? I should say not. She worships him. Keeps asking me when "nice man" is coming back.'

Damaris gave up. 'Nice' wasn't a word she had ever been much inclined to associate with Joel, certainly not in connection with Ginny whom up until now he had ignored. But if her daughter was content, then so was she—for the moment.

Fifteen minutes later to the second Joel reappeared in the doorway carrying Ginny.

'How did you get in?' asked Damaris, as it occurred to her that not only had he walked into her room without knocking, he had apparently also walked into her house.

'Through the door,' he replied innocently.

Damaris sighed. 'Yes, but wasn't it locked?'

'It was. I have a key.'

'But how. . .?'

'Your friend Chloe gave it to me, remember?'

'Oh. And you didn't return it,' she said.

He grinned. 'I did not. You never know when keys may come in handy. As in this case.'

It was hard to argue with that in view of the fact that he'd apparently saved the day after her untimely collapse on the floor. So she didn't bother.

'Mama,' said Ginny, beaming. 'Mama. . .' She jabbed her finger at Joel's cheek. 'Nice man.'

Damaris raised her eyes and found that her head still ached. 'This is an astounding reversal,' she observed. Her low voice was weak, but the old teasing note was back. 'Before I ended up in this state, my daughter refused to call you anything, and tended to give you the sort of look she usually reserves for cold spinach.'

'I noticed. We've come to an understanding since then, haven't we, Ginny?'

Ginny giggled as he lifted her on to his shoulder, where she wound her chubby fingers in his hair.

'Ouch,' he protested, screwing up his face and making Ginny giggle even harder.

Damaris smiled and held out her arms. 'My turn,' she said.

'Better not,' said Nurse Johnston, swooping across the room to seize the child. 'You may still be infectious, Mrs Gordon. I'd advise you to wait a few days before getting too close to your little girl. Come along, dear, we'll go fix Mama some breakfast.' She took Ginny's hand. 'You can mix the eggs.'

'Eggs,' agreed Ginny, who at first had looked close to rebellion at being separated from her brand new idol.

'Will I do instead?' asked Joel, taking a quick step across the room and dropping down on to the bed. 'You can hug me, if you like.'

'I probably should,' she replied. 'Those roses are from you, aren't they? I also have a feeling that without your intervention I'd be in very bad shape indeed. What happened, Joel? How did you happen to arrive at the right moment? Why did you arrive at all, come to that?'

'Because I'd had some time to get over wanting to murder you, and decided that since what I actually wanted to do was make love to you I'd better do something about it.'

'Oh.' She smiled weakly. 'I'm afraid I wasn't up to it. Was it a great disappointment?'

'It was more than a disappointment, my girl. You scared the hell out of me.' He put out a hand and gently smoothed back her hair. 'I heard on the radio that houses in this area had been hit by lightning and that occupants might have been injured. They weren't giving out any details so I came over at once and of course found that the house was still standing, but its owner wasn't. To make matters worse, your daughter had managed to clamber out of her cot and was sitting on top of you crying.'

'Oh, poor Ginny.'

'Apart from being hungry and very wet, poor Ginny was in much better condition than her mother. So after I'd got you to bed and called the doctor I cleaned her up and got her something to eat.'

'You mean you bathed her?'

'And changed her. Don't sound so surprised. I've had a lot of practice, remember.'

'Oh. And you knew what to feed her?'

'Not entirely. The care and feeding of infants has changed somewhat since my child-minding days. Ginny showed me.'

'She would.'

'Mm. And that calico-coloured feline of yours also showed a marked interest in food, and seemed to know exactly where I'd find it. She hasn't been giving me the evil eye nearly as frequently lately—although I must say Nurse Johnston and I had quite a time convincing her she couldn't set up housekeeping on your sick-bed.'

'Oh,' said Damaris again, overwhelmed by this changed state of affairs. 'Oh, Joel, thank you. I don't know what would have happened if you hadn't turned up when you did.'

He turned away from her. 'Neither do I,' he said huskily. 'And don't you *ever* think of doing that to me again.'

Damaris put up her hand to touch his cheek. 'I won't if I can help it,' she assured him.

Joel caught her wrist and pressed his lips into her palm. 'You'd better help it,' he said roughly.

'Joel, Nurse says I may still be infectious.'

'To hell with Nurse. And anyway, wasps are always infectious.'

'I don't think they are. . .' Damaris started to argue, but her words were cut off as he put his arms round her shoulders and lifted her up against his chest.

'Really, Mr Agar,' said a disapproving voice from the door. 'Mrs Gordon needs to be handled very carefully——'

'I am handling her carefully,' Joel assured her. 'Like spun glass.'

'I don't break that easily,' murmured Damaris from the depths of his shirt.

'No, I don't believe you do. Come on, let's get these pillows up behind you. Nurse has your breakfast.'

A few minutes later Nurse Johnston, still looking disapproving, had been chivvied out of the room by Joel, who was once more sitting on the edge of the bed as he tried to spoon scrambled eggs into Damaris's reluctant mouth.

'You're acting like a mother bird, Joel,' she grumbled. 'I can feed myself.'

'All right, go ahead.' He relinquished the spoon and sat back.

Damaris tried to pick it up and found that she wasn't nearly as strong as she had thought. It rattled crazily against the edge of the plate.

He smiled complacently, took it back, and continued with what Damaris was mentally dubbing 'operation mother-hen'.

When the eggs had been consumed she found she was surprisingly tired again, and Joel went away soon afterwards, after laying her gently back against the pillows. She was vaguely conscious that he was back that evening, and several times the following day, when he appeared beside her bed for just long enough to tell her to get some more rest. But it wasn't until two days later that she felt strong enough to come to grips with the startling fact that Joel, whom she had rejected forever, among other reasons because he didn't care for her daughter, now seemed to be the centre of Ginny's universe, the one whose advent she awaited as eagerly as most children waited for Christmas. Only Joel arrived more often than once a year.

'Joel,' she said, frowning, when he sat down on her bed on Monday evening after dropping a quick kiss on her forehead. 'Joel, I thought you said you didn't *like* children. . .?'

'I said something to the effect that as a general rule I don't like children,' he agreed. 'But it's not dislike really. Just over-exposure when I was much too young to appreciate the delights of child-rearing.'

'Mm.' Damaris stared doubtfully up at his face and wondered about the sardonic little gleam in his eye. 'Ginny thinks you're God.'

'Then I'm afraid she'll be disillusioned sooner or later.'

'Yes, but. . . Joel, do you like Ginny?'

'As a matter of fact,' he replied, the sardonic gleam even more pronounced, 'I have to admit, I've become very attached to that little blonde demon in angel's clothing. She reminds me a lot of her mother. She's not unlike my sister either, and I always found her easier to put up with than my brothers. Besides. . .' he grinned self-mockingly '. . .although I'm used to being regarded as the devil, it's been a while since anyone looked on me as God. I think I find it rather soothing.'

'Soothing,' scoffed Damaris. 'Oh, Joel.'

His features softened. 'Did it matter so much then, wasp? I didn't realise. . .no, didn't *think*, I guess. Was *that* why you shot away from me as if I were Jack the Ripper heading out for an evening's entertainment—that night before I went away?'

'It had something to do with it,' admitted Damaris.

'I see. And now? I hope you're not still hell-bent on pushing me out of your life. Because I warn you, I'm not about to go.'

'Oh,' said Damaris, glad to have the decision taken out of her hands for the moment. 'In that case there's not much point in my pushing, is there?'

'None at all.' He planted another firm kiss on her forehead, and left her to the mercies of Nurse Johnston, who was advancing with tea and a thermometer.

Three days later Damaris, wearing a canary-yellow robe, was seated peacefully in the living-room watching Ginny, who as usual was heading for the wood basket. Joel, seated opposite, was also watching the little girl.

'Leave it, Ginny,' he said quietly—and, to Damaris's amazement, Ginny left it.

'You're a miracle-worker,' she exclaimed.

'No, just the eldest of several brothers.'

He smiled, and now that she was feeling better Damaris was acutely aware of the devastating effect of that smile.

'How would you like a little holiday from the blonde terror there?' he asked now, nodding at Ginny.

'Holiday? But I can't——'

'Yes, you can. You'll be right as rain in another week, and Nurse Johnston has agreed to stay on to take care of Little Miss Trouble.'

'How do you know? I haven't asked her.'

'No, but I have.'

'Joel, you've no *right*. . .' Damaris had a sudden sensation that everything was back to normal as she felt a familiar indignation at his high-handedness. 'No right at all——'

'I know.' He smiled with infuriating smugness. 'Have you ever known that to stop me?'

'No,' she admitted. 'But that doesn't mean——'

'As a matter of fact, Mrs Gordon,' he said softly, reaching across to place two fingers beneath her chin, 'it means you're coming to New York with me next week.'

CHAPTER SEVEN

'NEW YORK,' gasped Damaris. 'I am *not* going to New York with you, Joel.'

'Yes, you are,' he replied equably. 'It's all arranged.'

'Then un-arrange it.'

'Not on your life. This is business—among other things.'

'Fine, then you don't need me——'

'Yes, I do. Stop arguing with me, Damaris. It's a very bad habit, of which I intend to cure you quite swiftly.'

'Like hell you do. Joel, I don't *want* to go to New York.'

'Why not?'

'Well, because. . .' She hesitated.

'Because I didn't ask you nicely? Is that it?'

The only answer he received was a venomous glare.

'All right, I'll try again.' He smiled, with provoking patience. 'Damaris, will you come to New York with me next week, because I should very much enjoy your company, because it's time you had a holiday, and because you told me once that you'd never had much chance to travel?'

When Damaris still said nothing, he added resignedly, 'Please?'

She raised her eyes, which had been sullenly fixed on the floor.

He was lounging back in the armchair with his legs stretching endlessly in front of him. His pale grey shirt exposed the upper part of his chest, and his hands were

loosely linked behind his neck. He was also grinning—
the most annoying, knowing, seductive grin that
Damaris had ever seen in her life.

She tried to fight it, tugged firmly at the tie of her
robe, swallowed hard and clamped her lips together.
None of it did any good.

With a little gurgle that eventually turned into a laugh,
she gave up completely. 'All right,' she agreed, defeated.
'You win again. If it really is OK with Nurse Johnston,
I'll go with you. On one condition.'

'I was afraid you'd say that.'

'You don't know what I was going to say.'

'Yes, I do. You were going to tell me your one
condition is that I don't get any ideas about enjoying
your delightful body along with your charming company,
and that you expect this to be a strictly platonic
arrangement.'

'Yes,' said Damaris sweetly. 'That's it exactly.'

Joel shook his head. 'Disgraceful ingratitude,' he
reproved her. 'And what if I don't accept your terms,
Mrs Gordon?'

Did that slight emphasis on the 'Mrs' mean that he
didn't see what she thought she was defending? Well,
that was just too bad.

'If you don't accept,' she said quite pleasantly, 'then I
haven't the slightest intention of going with you. And if
all your kindness this past week has been an elaborate
rite of seduction, it's original and very impressive. But it
won't work.'

Joel shook his head again. 'An ungrateful *and* sus-
picious wasp,' he said reproachfully. 'But as you don't
leave me much choice—I accept.'

From then on, as Nurse Johnston and the doctor had
predicted, Damaris's recovery was rapid. By the end of

the week she was her normal, healthy self, although, as Joel did not hesitate to point out, she could have used a little fattening up.

'I'm not a turkey,' she objected.

'That's debatable.'

'Well, of all the. . .' She struggled for words, gave up searching for just the right put-down, and shoved him none-too-gently in the chest. 'If you're going to start being critical again,' she grumbled, 'you can go straight back home and stay there.'

As he was on the doorstep at the time, and just about to leave anyway, this threat didn't have as much effect as it might have, so he kissed her smartly on the lips and departed.

Damaris spent the weekend packing two suitcases, then unpacking them again and rushing out to the shops to buy a whole new wardrobe. She spent Monday disrupting Nurse Johnston's routine with a million last-minute instructions about the care and feeding of Ginny, and only stopped when the beleaguered woman, exasperated, told her that as she'd been taking care of the child single-handedly for the past two weeks there really wasn't any reason to doubt her competence.

Shamefaced, Damaris apologised and went to re-pack her cases.

On Tuesday Joel's secretary, a tall young man, drove them out to the airport and assisted them as far as the gates.

'You don't have your own private jet then?' remarked Damaris to Joel, her tone mildly sarcastic. She had noticed that, even without private transport, they seemed to get through the red tape much faster than less privileged passengers.

'Not yet. I'm thinking about it,' replied Joel offhandedly.

Damaris gulped. She had meant the remark as a gibe.

It was a smooth flight, the first she had ever taken because Scott hadn't let her accompany him on business trips, claiming she wouldn't fit in with his colleagues. He hadn't taken her on holidays either, saying that, as she no longer worked, her life was one long holiday anyway.

It was strange sitting here miles above the ground with Joel beside her, being waited on by a bevy of efficient and, in this case, deferential attendants. It was strange just being with Joel, almost as if this was her rightful place. And she enjoyed the feeling, enjoyed his quiet conversation and easy silences. There wasn't any need to talk now, because once again, just as it had been on the *Jacqueline* she felt utterly relaxed and comfortable with this man.

After a while he took her hand and held it loosely against the fine fabric stretching across his thigh—and that felt right too.

It was almost a disappointment when the plane touched down at Kennedy Airport, and after that it seemed no time at all before they were installed in a limousine and speeding towards New York's best-known hotel.

'I've booked adjoining suites,' explained Joel as the bellboy escorted them along a hallway. When he saw her glance up at him sharply, he added in a voice that was drier than sand in the desert, 'Yes, there's a communicating door, but you can lock it.'

'I will,' Damaris assured him.

Five minutes later she was alone in her palatial suite,

staring down at the City of New York. Joel had thought-fully accounted for her fear of heights so they were only six storeys up, which meant the view was somewhat restricted. Even so, she felt a little flicker of excitement because at last she was going to experience a world that lay outside the province of British Columbia.

Joel had said he would give her time to rest and change before he collected her for dinner, so she hung up all her new clothes—though they were only staying for five days she'd managed to cram in enough for fifty—and lay back on the large double bed. Which immediately led her thoughts in the direction she'd been trying to avoid.

Why, if Joel had come back into her life specifically because he wanted to make love to her—and he had admitted as much—had he readily, if not enthusiasti-cally, agreed to her condition about a strictly platonic arrangement? For that matter, why had she made the condition?

Well that was easy, she thought, biting at the corner of her lip. She was just plain scared. In spite of the change in Joel's attitude to her daughter, she was still afraid of any involvement that might threaten her prized independence. She had tried to resist coming here with him, but Joel, with his usual hurricane-force persuasion, had somehow bowled over her objections and got her to do what he wanted. What *she* wanted too, if she was honest.

She glanced at her watch and sat up. Time to think about bathing and changing. But, as she ran the water into the luxurious pink jacuzzi, she knew she hadn't answered her main question. Why had Joel wanted her to come? She shied away from the obvious conclusion—that he had never had any intention of honouring her conditions—and let the gently steaming waters soothe her body. But nothing could relax her mind, she realised as the soft vibrations penetrated her skin. She sighed. All right, so she would live for the moment and let the future take care of itself.

After she had enjoyed a leisurely soak and changed into an elegant but comfortable petal-peach dress with thin shoulder-straps and a softly pleated skirt, there was just time to phone Nurse Johnston to check on Ginny before Joel arrived at her door—the one leading to the hallway, not the carefully locked one between their suites.

As always, the moment she saw him Damaris felt a curl of delicious tension at the magnificent figure he made in evening dress. It seemed to accentuate that aura of power that was never far from the surface with this man. Funny; normally she found powerful arrogant men unattractive. But that certainly wasn't the way she felt about this particular specimen of dominant masculinity.

She found him breathtaking.

His smile was breathtaking too as he took her hand and tucked it under his arm.

'Glamorous Damaris,' he teased her softly. 'That colour suits you.'

'Thank you,' she mumbled, wishing she didn't feel like a schoolgirl on her first date with the hero of the football team. It was infuriating that one compliment from him, combined with the feel of his body as he walked close beside her down the hall, should be making her feel weak and light-headed.

Things didn't get much better once she was seated across from him in the hotel's grand and glittering dining-room.

She had made conditions about this trip and he had accepted them, but if he continued to look at her in that way, all warm and sexy and seductive, she wasn't sure what might happen later. She moistened her lips and forced herself to look away from him.

Immediately, and with a devastating sense of shock, she ceased to be aware of his existence.

'What is it?' he asked. 'Have you seen a ghost?'

Damaris jumped and returned abruptly to the realisation that she was here in New York with Joel, not in Vancouver four years back with a very different kind of man.

'No,' she murmured, her low voice filled with distress. 'No. A ghost I could cope with. But Craig. . . Craig's no ghost.'

'Craig?' The word cracked like a gunshot.

'Yes. He's over there, across the room. With a party of businessmen, I think.'

'Very enlightening.'

His sarcasm pulled her out of the trance she had rapidly been falling into as the past caught up with the present and threatened to overwhelm her.

'I went out with Craig for a year,' she explained, not looking at him.

'I see.' His mouth curved unpleasantly. 'And I actually thought you'd been playing the grieving widow.'

Damaris shook her head, confused by the bitterness in his voice. 'No, you don't understand. Craig and I met at Gordon and Son's long before I was married. In fact I think he stayed on with the firm after I sold my share of the business.'

'Ah. An old flame then. But obviously not forgotten.'

They were interrupted by the arrival of champagne at that point, and Damaris had time to collect her thoughts.

When they were alone again she said quietly, 'It's not really any of your business, Joel. But I'll tell you about him if you like.'

'Oh, no,' he groaned. 'Revelations of a Reluctant Virgin. I'm not sure I can stand it.'

Damaris's fingers tightened on the stem of her glass.

'Don't do it,' he warned.

'No,' she replied, after a moment. 'I don't think I will. That remark wasn't worth the waste of good champagne.' Deliberately she picked up the glass, held it to the light and took a small, appreciative sip.

Joel glared at her, obviously fighting to control some emotion she couldn't, and didn't want to, understand. Then he said in a clipped, still angry voice, 'You're quite right. I apologise.'

Damaris nodded, wondering what had happened to this evening that had started out so well. 'Apology accepted,' she said wearily.

She watched Joel struggle with his pride, knowing what he wanted to ask but not helping.

He took a deep breath, the battle won. 'As you said, it's none of my business, Damaris. But yes, I would like to hear about your Craig. Any man who can make those grey eyes of yours go so big and haunted must surely be worth something.'

'Not really. But I thought so at one time. I thought I was in love with him too, even though he always had to have everything *his* way. My foster-father was like that, of course, so I thought it was normal. Our relationship ended because Scott began to take an interest in me.'

Joel's eyes narrowed to slits. 'You mean you ditched your love for a bigger and better fish?'

Damaris bit her lip. 'Joel, what's the matter with you tonight? Why are you treating me like. . .like some kind of dirt beneath your elegant feet?' She felt her eyes misting, and knew that if she didn't burst into tears she was liable to hit him over the head with the nearest blunt instrument; in this case, a plateful of artichoke salad which the waiter had just placed in front of her.

Joel closed his eyes briefly. 'I'm sorry.' He picked up a bread stick and snapped it between his fingers. 'I don't know what's the matter with me. Go on.'

Damaris glanced across the room and saw that Craig and his party were leaving. Thank goodness for that. And he hadn't seen her.

'All right,' she said tiredly. 'If you'd given me a chance I was going to tell you that when Scott started showing an interest Craig started seeing dollar signs. He said I should encourage Scott, get as much money out of him as possible. Maybe even marry him if I could. Then a couple of years later, he said, I could get a divorce and the two of us could live on my alimony, which he expected would run into millions. It wouldn't have, of course. Scott was very comfortable, but not in the million-dollar-settlement class.' When Joel seemed about to say something, she went on quickly, 'No, that wasn't why I married Scott. I was horrified, disillusioned—and very hurt when I discovered how unscrupulous Craig was. We had one last terrible scene—and that was the end of that. But I doubt if he's ever forgiven me.'

'Forgiven *you*? What are you talking about?' Joel looked as if he was searching for something to smash.

'Don't people always blame others when they're shown up as less than commendable? Craig's no exception.'

'I see.' Joel looked around. 'Where is he?'

'He's gone. Why?'

'Too bad. And because he sounds like a man who needs his butt kicked, that's why.' He passed his hand over his eyes, then looked at her and said with quiet sincerity, 'I'm sorry, wasp. Forgive me. I should have known.'

She was puzzled. 'Known what?'

'That you're much too nice to be a user of other people. Hell, I've probably been more guilty of that than you have over the years.'

'Not necessarily,' said Damaris, not wanting to unearth any more skeletons. 'I'm no angel, Joel. As you've pointed out on several occasions.'

'So I have,' he replied, smiling crookedly. 'How could I have forgotten?'

Damaris smiled back and said nothing, hoping he would change the subject. But he didn't.

'One thing,' he said slowly, snapping another bread stick, 'You did marry Scott in the end. Was that. . .on the rebound?'

'I suppose it was in a way. I was—numb, for a long time after Craig. But that wasn't the whole story.'

'Want to tell me?'

'No,' said Damaris quickly. 'No, I don't want to talk about the past any more. It's over.'

'Just so long as it is.' He leaned forward and placed his hand over hers where it rested on the edge of the table. 'I've been behaving atrociously this evening, haven't I? I shouldn't have asked.'

She waved her free hand dismissively. 'No, you shouldn't, but, as I think you once said to me, when has that ever stopped you?'

He grinned. 'Until I met you, never.'

The main course came soon after that, and the rest of the meal passed easily in pleasant, inconsequential conversation. Damaris was pleased to note that Joel seemed to be making a special effort to make up for his earlier harshness.

Afterwards they had coffee, and suddenly she found she was very tired.

'If you don't mind,' she said, not quite meeting his

eyes, 'it's been a long day, and I think I'd like to go to bed now.'

'So would I,' he agreed, picking up her hand and touching it to his lips. His amber eyes gleamed at her over the top of her knuckles.

'Alone,' she said firmly.

'Are you sure?'

'Quite sure.'

He sighed. 'Whoever gave women the idea that they have any business knowing their own minds?'

Damaris laughed. 'Women have always known their own minds, my friend. It's about time you men accepted that.'

'I do accept. Under protest.'

For a moment, when they paused outside the door of her room, Damaris wasn't sure he'd accepted anything, because suddenly he caught her around the shoulders, moved his hands achingly slowly down her spine, and covered her mouth with his lips. His tongue explored the moist sweetness, firmly, explicitly, drawing a response from her that she hadn't wanted to give. Then his hands moved even lower, covering her bottom as she strained towards him—and abruptly he forced her against him so that she couldn't escape the knowledge of his arousal. His hips ground erotically into hers, making her gasp, and at once Joel raised his head and murmured thickly, 'I want you, Damaris. One day I'm going to have you.'

He was gazing down at her, his bronzed skin very dark. His eyes were dark too, and they held a question.

When she didn't answer it, but only stared up at him, mesmerised, he spun her sharply around, unlocked the door, gave her a smart pat on the bottom and pushed her into her room.

'Goodnight, Damaris,' he said very softly.

As she heard the door close behind him, she could still feel the delicious tingle where his hand had been.

Later, as she pulled the covers around her in the very large bed meant for two, she remembered how she had assured him that women always knew their own minds. Well, at the moment she wasn't at all sure that she knew hers. Joel wanted her, and he had said he would have her eventually. Perhaps he would. But not now. Not yet. Because the only thing she was sure of at this moment was that once that step had been taken her life would be irrevocably changed. After that there could be no turning back.

She glanced at the locked door between their rooms, thought with a strange wistfulness of Joel, and wondered if he too was staring at that door; and then, within seconds, she wasn't thinking of anything as the long, exhausting day caught up with her and she fell asleep.

The next morning Joel arrived at her door almost on top of a breakfast tray set for two.

'I took the liberty of ordering for both of us,' he explained, pulling out a chair from the table as if he belonged in the room. 'Is this all right?' He gestured at the plate of bacon and eggs.

'Perfectly,' replied Damaris, thinking that if this was the only liberty he took she'd be lucky. Or unlucky, depending on how one looked at it.

At the moment Joel was looking at her rather pointedly, and she realised that in her haste to open the door she hadn't stopped to put on a robe. Oh, dear. Her nightgown wasn't exactly see-through, but it was made of a very light white cotton. As she hurried across the room to the cupboard she was conscious that Joel's eyes were following her, enjoying every revealing step she took.

'What did you have to do that for?' he asked as she struggled into her robe and tightened the belt.

'So that I can enjoy my breakfast without feeling as if I'm likely to be the next course,' said Damaris bluntly.

'I *was* enjoying mine,' he responded glumly. 'You're a spoil-sport as well as a wasp, Damaris Gordon.'

'Aren't I?' she agreed blandly, taking a delicate bite of her toast.

Joel, already dressed for the day's business, watched her with a small, appreciative smile.

When they had finished he explained that, as he would be tied up in meetings for most of the day, he'd arranged for a driver to show her around New York.

'Oh, no,' said Damaris quickly, 'I'll be fine on my own. I can take a bus or the subway.'

'You will not be fine on your own. Or at any rate, *I* won't be fine thinking about you on your own. Which is why Mortimer will be keeping an eye on you.'

'I don't need keeping an eye on. I'm not a child.'

'Precisely.'

There was something very inflexible about that, and as his eyes met hers she discovered, not for the first time, that this was a man who was used to being obeyed. She also saw something else. At first she wasn't sure what it was but after a while she realised that it was honest concern. Was he still thinking about Craig, then? she wondered suddenly; Craig, who was probably still in New York and quite possibly in this very hotel. Hm. Perhaps, after all, Joel had a point.

'Oh, all right,' she agreed grudgingly. 'If it will keep you happy. . .'

'It will. And I'm delighted to hear that my happiness is of some concern,' he said drily.

Damaris stopped feeling irritated and began to smile.

'Don't sound so stuffy,' she retorted, unable to repress a giggle.

'Stuffy?' he said, very softly. 'Is that what you think?' The light of retaliation glinted in his eye as he stood up and moved deliberately round the table.

'What are you doing?' she gulped as he removed the coffee cup from her clutching fingers and, taking her by the elbows, drew her up on to her feet.

'This,' he replied, bending to kiss her. At the same time his hands moved to the front of her robe.

'Well?' he asked, some minutes later, after completing a competent and thorough exploration that left every part of her body feeling scorched. 'Was that stuffy?'

'I. . .you. . .' Damaris was incapable of speech.

'Not sure? Shall I try again?'

'No,' she gasped, finding her voice and backing away from him. 'You'll be late for your meeting.'

'I think I could live with that,' he drawled, beginning to take off his jacket.

'Joel! No!' Damaris ran towards him, pulled wildly at the jacket and tried to push him out of the door.

He stood, rock-like, looking down at her with an amused little gleam in his eye. '"A" for effort,' he remarked when she couldn't move him. 'Why don't you pick on someone your own size?'

Damaris stopped pushing to glare at him, feeling thoroughly foolish. Joel merely smiled, rumpled her hair and when he reached the door turned round to say matter-of-factly, 'I'll be back about five, and Mortimer will be here to pick you up at ten. Don't keep him waiting.'

Once again Damaris looked round for something to throw at him, then remembered that the last time she had lost her temper to that extent she'd been a child.

And the consequences had been painful. In any case, Joel had already closed the door.

Don't keep him waiting, indeed! Who did he think he was, telling her how to behave? She sank back into the chair he had pulled her out of, her body sagging; and after some time her lips parted in a reluctant grin. Joel didn't *think* he was anyone. He knew he was Joel Agar, successful tycoon, breaker of women's hearts and, underneath all that glitter, a man who could be kind and gentle, who could make her laugh. He also happened to be the man she loved.

Shaking her head, Damaris began to get ready, and by five to ten she was dressed in a short-sleeved cotton jumpsuit and waiting for Mortimer to call.

Six and a half hours later, after a day that was exciting, exhausting, fascinating and very hot, she had seen more of New York than anyone should see in one day—with the notable exception of the city's Empire State Building, which, she had assured Mortimer, looked very nice from the bottom—and was back in the lobby of the hotel.

She looked at her watch. Four-thirty. Plenty of time for a shower before Joel got back. She was standing behind a pillar and just as she moved away from it to head for the lifts someone grabbed her arm from behind, and the one voice she didn't want to hear exclaimed loudly, 'Damaris! I don't believe it. What in heaven's name are you doing in this part of the world?'

Damaris closed her eyes and stifled a groan. 'Hello, Craig,' she replied, not turning around.

But at once he grabbed her other arm and swung her to face him. 'What's the matter?' he demanded. 'Aren't you pleased to see me?'

'Should I be?' she asked coldly, looking up into a lean, rather predatory face that hadn't changed much in four years. Still the silver-blond, Norse-god looks, and only a few lines round the eyes to mark the passage of time.

'Of course you should,' he bellowed. 'Heavens, Scott's been dead for years. . .'

'One and a half.'

'All right, one and a half. But that little disagreement we had; surely that's all forgotten? Listen, I'm here on business for Gordon's, and you're an independent woman of means now, I hear. We could have fun together. We can be friends again, can't we?'

'No,' said Damaris. 'We can't.'

'Oh, come *on*. . .'

'Craig, I may be a woman of means which you'd like to get your hands on, but I meant what I said that last day. I didn't want to see you again then. I still don't.'

He showed no signs of letting go of her arm, so now she pulled away from him and started to walk briskly across the lobby.

She had only taken a few steps when he caught up with her.

'Damaris. . .'

She kept on walking.

'Damaris, for goodness' sake.' A vice-like hand descended on her shoulder, forcing her to a stop and almost making her fall over. Craig's other hand shot out to steady her, and now both her shoulders were pinned in his long-fingered grip.

'Let go of me,' she said sharply.

'Only if you're nice to me.'

'Craig!' She tried to pull away but he wouldn't release her, and she saw that they were starting to attract the curious stares of passersby.

'I said let go,' she repeated loudly, hoping that the

attention they were receiving would force him to do as she demanded.

But it wasn't the amused attention of passing guests that had the desired effect; it was a very large hand that seized the back of Craig's collar. A hand that jerked him around like a limp doll as its owner aimed a purposeful fist in the direction of his well-shaped jaw.

'Joel!' screamed Damaris. 'Joel, don't!'

The fist was a hair's breadth away from connecting with flesh and bone. 'Why not?' he demanded in a voice that was shaking with fury.

'Because—please, Joel. Don't make a scene. I—it's all right now. Really. Just let him go.'

Craig's eyes darted sideways at her from a face that was white with uncertainty. Joel's face was white too, but with a rage so intense that it scared her. She'd never seen him come this close to losing control.

His fist was still inches from Craig's jaw, and short of flinging herself dramatically between them Damaris didn't know what to do to defuse the very real possibility of an undignified punch-up in the lobby of New York's best hotel.

'Please,' she repeated desperately.

Somehow that got through to him. Reluctantly, and only after shaking the much taller Craig as if he were a small and obnoxious dog, Joel released his panic-stricken captive.

Just in time, thought Damaris, offering up a silent prayer of thanks. Security was fast approaching on the left.

Craig didn't stay to try any further conclusions. Without a word, he scuttled behind a pillar and out of sight.

'Everything's under control,' growled Joel to the

suspicious-looking security officer who was about to put in his two cents' worth. 'Come on, Damaris.'

He took her arm and began to hustle her through the wide-eyed crowd so fast that again she almost fell. A little to her surprise, the security man shrugged and seemed to accept Joel's assurance, and the gaping but unconcerned onlookers parted in front of them as if they were visiting royalty.

Joel didn't say a word until they reached her room, and then he snapped the door shut behind them with so much force that it shuddered against its hinges.

Damaris wetted her lips and stared at him, not sure what was coming next as he leaned back against the wall with his hands rammed into his pockets and his powerful frame emitting an almost tangible rage. She could see the muscles pressing against the tightness of his shirt. . .

'Did he hurt you?' he rapped out. 'Because if he did——'

'No.' Damaris shook her head. 'No, he didn't. He was just being. . .a nuisance.' When Joel only stared at her with a curious hardness, she added quickly, 'I didn't encourage him, Joel. I was trying to make him go away.'

He shifted his shoulders impatiently. 'I could see that—and I should have messed up that pretty face of his as I intended. Why in hell did you stop me?'

'Oh, Joel. Craig's not worth making a scene over. And, knowing him, he'd have had you up for assault.'

'Let him. He'd have lost.'

'Maybe, but you're not invincible, you know.' She gave a little shiver and brushed a weary hand over her eyes. 'All the same, I'm so glad you came when you did. I'm even more glad it didn't go any further. I'm sure he won't bother me any more.'

Joel's fists bunched against his thighs. 'Believe me, he won't.'

He looked so furious still, so aggressively male, and as if he was just aching for a fight, that Damaris tried to smile brightly in order to lighten what seemed to her a lethally dangerous mood. She *tried* to smile—but found herself choking back a sob instead.

Immediately Joel was across the room and then his arms were around her and she was being held fast against his chest. 'It's all right, wasp,' he soothed, stroking her quivering shoulders. 'Don't cry on me. I didn't mean to make you cry. . .'

'You. . .d-didn't,' sniffed Damaris. 'You were wonderful. It's just that I w-wanted this evening to be so happy, and now you're angry. And I hated seeing Craig again, hated him touching me. . .' She gave up trying to restrain her tears and buried her face in his jacket.

'It's OK, sweetheart, it's OK,' he murmured, his lips just touching her hair. 'Here, come on. Sit down now and let me mop you up.'

He pushed her gently down on to the big bed and seated himself beside her. Then his hand was on the back of her head and he was patting a clean linen handerchief over her tear-stained cheeks.

She gave a last loud sniff and stopped crying. 'I'm sorry,' she whispered. 'I'm not usually such a boring waterworks.'

'You're not a boring waterworks. You're my very own, dear wasp. And I love you.'

'Wh-what?' Damaris raised big, swimming eyes, certain she must have heard wrongly.

'I said, I love you. You're impossible, maddening, and you drive me crazy, and I think that sting of yours must have turned my head—which hasn't stopped spinning since the day I met you.' He smiled ruefully. 'Why do you think I behaved like such a moron last night when I thought Craig still meant something to you? I was wild with jealousy, that's why. And when I saw that reptile's claws on you this afternoon I think if you hadn't stopped me I might have killed him. I still think it's an opportunity missed.'

Damaris smiled back wanly. 'That wouldn't have been very practical,' she murmured. 'Besides, I've never been the sort of woman who fancies being brawled over like some docile doe waiting to accept the stag with the toughest antlers. I prefer to make my own choices, thank you.' She sighed. 'Even if they've usually been wrong.'

'Mm.' Joel's eyes were hooded. 'I know about you and your choices. Damaris. . .?'

'Yes?'

He looked straight at her then, took both her hands and twined her fingers in his. 'Damaris, I've told you I love you——'

Her eyes widened, suddenly wary. 'Yes. Yes, you have, but. . .'

'But what?'

She took a quick, much-needed breath. 'Joel, are you saying that because it's true or—or because you think it may make me more. . .amenable?'

He frowned. 'Amenable? Oh, I see.'

From the quick flare of anger in his eyes, she thought for a moment that he meant to do her violence. But instead he gave her a long, steady look, tightened his hold on her fingers and said levelly, 'No, wasp. If I wanted to seduce you, I don't think I'd have to go to those lengths to make you amenable. I'm saying it because it's true. I want you to be my wife, Damaris Gordon.'

CHAPTER EIGHT

DAMARIS tried to swallow and couldn't because there was an odd sort of tightness in her throat. She tried to tear her eyes from Joel's, but she couldn't do that either because the intensity of his gaze held her pinioned.

'M-marry,' she finally managed to stutter. 'You want to *marry* me?'

'That's what I said.' He was smiling his old stomach-turning smile, but there were lines of strain around his mouth that hadn't been there before, and his eyes seemed guarded—waiting.

'Do you mean you want an answer—now?'

Her head was spinning just as he'd said his was. She felt as if every landmark by which she'd ever been guided had been snatched from her, leaving her dizzy and unprotected in some strange jungle of her own emotions. She loved this man, but up until now she had managed to convince herself that he only liked and wanted her. That way she felt safe; or as safe as she could ever feel with Joel. But now he was saying he loved her too, wanted to marry her—to trap her as she had once been trapped before, in a partnership that would probably turn out to be one-sided. His was such a forceful personality that the danger of losing her cherished independence was very real. On top of that, she had always been half convinced that his marriage to Sharon had ended the moment it had ceased to amuse him. That could happen to her too. But if she said no. . .

If she said no, then Joel could no longer have any part in her life.

He was still gripping her hands, but his eyes were no longer guarded. Now they had turned hard and demanding, so that she knew she was being forced to a decision. He wouldn't let her prevaricate any more. She had asked if he wanted an answer now, but that was an empty question.

'I. . . Joel, I can't. . . I don't know. . .' She was trying, but she couldn't keep her mind from skittering off in a hundred panicky directions.

'Don't you love me?'

Suddenly all her wayward thoughts were back in line, concentrated on what, at this moment, seemed to be the only thing in the world that mattered.

'Yes,' she said quietly, dropping her forehead against his chest. 'Yes, I do love you, Joel. Very much.'

She felt his fingers beneath her chin as he lifted her face up, and the blaze of relief in his eyes was so bright that it almost consumed her.

'Then you'll marry me.'

It wasn't a question at all. In fact it sounded more like an order. And that frightened her.

'I. . .don't know.'

'What do you mean, you don't know?' His hand clamped around her wrist. 'Damaris, don't be an idiot. I love you, you love me, and even if we drive each other crazy, which seems more than probable, we both know we can't be happy apart. I've known that since that day on the *Jacqueline* and so have you, whether we've admitted it or not.'

Damaris managed a watery smile. 'I suppose you're right—as usual. But, Joel, I've been married before——'

'So have I. What does that matter? I know you think I'm arrogant, and perhaps I am, but when have I ever demanded to be the first and only?'

'No,' said Damaris. 'No, you don't understand. You see—my marriage wasn't a very happy one, and when it ended I decided I'd never make a. . .a mistake like that again.'

'A mistake like what?'

'Well. . .like marrying.'

'Mm.' Joel placed his hands heavily on her shoulders, and his mouth twisted. 'I know. I made the same decision myself after Sharon.'

'Really?' She blinked. 'Did you? Then why. . .?'

'Because you're not Sharon. Thank goodness. And because if I can't have you I shall very probably murder you instead.'

'Oh.' Damaris thought about that, and smiled shakily. 'I'm not sure that homicide would help.'

'It would help to relieve my feelings,' he explained.

She frowned. 'Do you mean you're willing to marry me because you. . .*want* me?' Her voice was doubtful, not daring to trust.

'No, you infuriating, siren-voiced little fool.' He was practically roaring now. 'I am not *willing* to marry you. I *want* to marry you. And I intend to.'

'But I'm not sure. . .'

Joel raised resigned eyes to the high white ceiling. 'Obviously I'll have to make you sure then, won't I?' He grinned, and it was such a suggestive grin that her stomach started turning cartwheels.

Then, as she gaped at him, hypnotised, he put both arms round her waist to draw her against him. She could feel the hardness of his chest through her cotton jump-suit, smell the intoxicating masculine scent of him. . .and his lips were on hers, and somehow she was lying back on the covers with his body heavy on top of her. His lean, trousered thigh was between her legs. She felt his fingers at her neck as the narrow zip of her jumpsuit slid slowly and very deliberately to her waist.

'Joel,' she murmured, her arms creeping around his neck to push beneath the collar of his jacket. In a moment the jacket was on the floor, along with his tie, and then he was back beside her, running tantalising fingers down her sides.

'Come here,' he murmured, pulling her to him so that the length of her body was blissfully entwined with his. As every part of her lit with an agonising need, he began a slow, stroking exploration of her breasts, her thighs, her stomach, and all of her that he could hold within his hands.

But he made no effort to remove the jumpsuit, and just when she thought she could bear the waiting no longer, and as her straining body screamed at him for release, quite suddenly he lifted her eager fingers from his belt, held her away from him, and sat up.

'Well?' he said, eyes very bright and gleaming as he loomed above her with his palms pressed flat on either side of her head. 'Are you sure now?'

'I'm sure I want you,' moaned Damaris, her pulses still racing and her heart still thundering against her ribs. 'But I suppose I always knew that.'

Joel's face darkened and abruptly he stood up. As she stared at him, stupefied, he strode across the room to the window. 'I see,' he said with his back to her. 'You want me, you love me, but you don't want to marry me. Is that what you're trying to say?'

Damaris felt tears prick her eyes again, as she reached

blindly for Joel's sodden handkerchief. It had disappeared.

'I don't know what I'm trying to say,' she answered with painful honesty. 'I'm so—so confused.'

'Apparently. You're not the only one.'

'Joel, please, try to understand. . .'

He swung round at that to glare down at her from what seemed an intimidating height. His hands grasped the window sill behind him and he looked to Damaris like a tiger about to pounce on its prey. 'I am trying to understand,' he growled. 'You don't make it easy.'

She eyed him warily, decided her current position put her at a definite disadvantage, and sat up, at the same time restoring her zip to its rightful place. 'If you'll listen instead of snarling at me every time I open my mouth, I'll try to explain,' she told him, not wanting to inflame him further but knowing that if she didn't speak forcefully he was in no mood to pay much attention.

She saw his chest expand as he took a deep breath and made a visible effort to control his obvious frustration.

'All right. I'm listening,' he said curtly.

Damaris sincerely hoped he was. 'You see,' she began, pushing a stray wisp of hair out of her eyes, 'all the time I was growing up I was dependent on other peoples' not very charitable charity. My one dream was to escape from that, and when I did of course I had only myself to depend on. I managed, but for me independence turned out to be synonymous with insecurity. I had very little money and no one to turn to but myself. Then I got the job at Gordon's, and things were a little better financially. And I met Craig. For the first time in my life I thought I had someone who really cared what happened to me.' She tugged at her expanding watchband, making it snap, and added flatly, 'But I was wrong. Then I became Scott's secretary, and things were even better money-wise, but there was still very little left over after I'd paid rent for my one-room apartment and bought food, and made sure I was dressed presentably for the job. In the end, of course, Scott asked me to marry him. I couldn't believe it. We'd been out a few times but I'd never thought his intentions, unlike Craig's, were remotely serious. I was his secretary, and it seemed natural to have supper together sometimes—after work.'

'And after that all your worries were over,' taunted Joel, who was looking at her with a kind of bitter scepticism that she couldn't even begin to understand.

'No,' said Damaris. 'They might have been if I'd loved Scott. But I didn't.'

'And that mattered?' His face became oddly still as he waited for her to reply.

'Yes, it did. He was much older than me, of course, but I wanted to love him. After all, he was the answer to a prayer. As his wife, I'd have someone who cared about me at last—and I'd never have to be insecure again, emotionally or financially.'

Joel's eyes narrowed. 'But you did marry him. What happened to all your scruples?'

She sighed. 'I took care of them by telling him the truth. I wasn't thinking straight at the time because I. . . I hadn't properly got over the shock of finding out that Craig wasn't. . .wasn't the man I thought he was. Anyway, I admitted to Scott that I didn't love him, but I said I'd try to be a good wife to him if he still wanted me.' She darted a quick look at Joel's set face and went on resolutely, 'In so many cultures people marry for practical reasons and learn to love each other later. I hoped it would be that way with us. But Scott went all cold and quiet and said that naturally that would suit him very well. His father had just died, he was taking over the presidency, and he felt that it was time he settled down to start a family. If I was willing to oblige in that line he'd be satisfied.'

'And he didn't mean a word of it,' said Joel harshly, 'did he?'

Damaris stared at him, surprised and puzzled. 'No. In retrospect, I think that was his way of saving face. He didn't love me, but I filled a need at the time, and he thought I'd be biddable and grateful. I *was* grateful. The trouble was, he was incredibly possessive, and although he didn't love me—he didn't love anyone but himself really—he resented the fact that I couldn't love him. It infuriated him that he could possess my body, my affection, even, but not my. . .my starstruck love. He thought he was God's gift to women, you see, because he was handsome. In the end he took out his frustrations by belittling me, saying I was too unsophisticated to mingle with his friends or be taken to parties. He was partly right. On one occasion when he did take me to a party I was so anxious to please him for once that in the end I was utterly tongue-tied——'

Joel made a sound that was a cross between a snort and a crack of derisive laughter, and Damaris heaved a weary sigh and said bleakly, 'You can laugh if you like, but it's true. I spent the entire evening covered in blushes.' She paused. 'I've changed since those days, learned that I don't have to let anyone push me around. In a way they never have, I suppose, but I was always too anxious to please——'

Joel gave another snort, but Damaris only gritted her teeth and continued.

'Not surprisingly, Scott flatly refused to take me out after that, and, anyway, by then I was pregnant and felt so fat and heavy that I didn't mind. So I stayed home a lot and gardened and read when I wasn't doing volunteer work. . .and because Scott didn't like me seeing the friends I'd made since I'd moved some of them stopped coming around. Then Ginny came and that made everything worse because he'd wanted a boy, to be the next president of Gordon's. He insisted that Ginny was all my fault—that I was too much of a child to have a boy.'

'Then he didn't know much about human biology, did he?' said Joel caustically. 'As to the rest of it, I feel sorry for him. It's not—I don't imagine it was much fun being married to a woman-child who had married him strictly for his money.'

Damaris flinched at the harsh judgement, not understanding why Joel, who had been so kind lately, had suddenly turned cruelly cold and hard. It made no sense when only a few minutes ago his eyes had been alight with love and he had been saying he wanted—no, *intended*—to marry her.

'Not just for his money,' she corrected, staring down at the dusty pink carpet. 'I wanted someone of my own too, someone to care about, even if I wasn't in love. And I wanted children.'

'And I suppose you thought that was enough?' The contempt in his voice was like a hard slap in her face.

'I hoped it would be,' she replied with quiet dignity. 'But of course it wasn't. I should never have married him. I didn't understand it at the time, but he wanted a much younger wife just to prove to himself and the world that he wasn't getting older like everyone else. In the end that's what killed him, his crazy obsession with youth. He wasn't trying to prove anything to me. He was proving his eternal youth to himself, and he'd been like that since long before I met him.'

'Fascinating. And why are you telling me all this now, may I ask?'

She winced at the lack of warmth in his tone. 'Because I want you to understand, Joel. I was devastated when Scott was killed because I knew I hadn't made his last years happy. I don't suppose anyone could have, but I still regretted it.'

'On the other hand, you had all that money to ease the pain, hadn't you? Security with no strings attached. Quite a coup.'

'Joel!' Damaris jumped up to face him. 'Joel, don't sound so—so contemptuous. You've always known I inherited Scott's estate. I'm trying to explain to you that after he died I decided I wouldn't ever marry again, because by then I knew how a marriage entered into with only honesty and good intentions can so easily turn into a nightmare—for both parties. And as you so kindly pointed out, I had security and independence—and my daughter. Everything I needed. Why rock the boat?'

'You've forgotten something,' said Joel grimly. 'You mentioned money and independence, and your daughter. But what about love, Damaris? Or perhaps I ought to say—sex.'

Damaris felt the blood rush hotly into her face. 'What are you accusing me of, Joel? That's what I've been trying to tell you. When I made that vow to stay single, it never occurred to me that I would ever fall deeply in love. As for sex, I may have had a child, but until I met you I—I don't think I even knew what it was all about. Not really.' She tried to smile. 'I guess I'm a late bloomer.' When he didn't smile back or respond in any way, she went on desperately, 'Don't you see, Joel? I do love you, but I've become so used to being independent, to thinking of myself as a contented single mother, that

I've been running away from even the thought of marriage. That's why I was confused when you asked me. Why I wasn't sure. I—I'm still not sure.'

She held out her hand, her smoky eyes beseeching, searching for reassurance in the uncompromising harshness of his features.

She didn't find it. 'I'm not sure either,' he replied, his voice as bleak as sleet on a winter's day. 'Perhaps we've both made a mistake.'

Damaris felt as if she'd just been stabbed to the heart. She had been trying so hard to make him understand her reluctance, why she needed time to think, and now he was telling her that perhaps, after all, she needn't bother. That, on second thoughts, he'd changed his mind.

Why? What had she done other than tell him the truth? Gradually, in the midst of her hurt and bewilderment, pride came to the rescue and she felt indignation stirring, a recurrence of the old suspicion and anger that had never been far from the surface in her dealings with Joel.

'You're right,' she snapped. 'I think we did make a mistake. Or at any rate, I did.' She drew herself up to her full, not very impressive height. 'Never mind—it's not too late to mend it. I said before you went away that it was time to end this little interlude. I let you talk me out of it once, but I won't again. Thank you for the holiday, Joel, but I think I'd better be on my way tomorrow. I'll have dinner in my room, if you don't mind.' She gave him a brilliant smile and extended her hand briskly, 'Goodbye, Joel.'

At first he continued to lean against the window sill with his hands in his pockets, not moving a muscle. His shoulders were hunched forward as he scowled at her from beneath lids that seemed even heavier than usual.

He looked incredibly weary all of a sudden, grim-visaged and with evening stubble beginning to darken his jaw. After a while he gave an almost imperceptible shrug, and without changing his expression took her outstretched hand and shook it briefly, as if he were concluding a rather unsatisfactory business transaction.

'Goodbye, Damaris,' he said bleakly. 'I'll arrange your flight.'

'Oh, no, you won't,' she snapped, still buoyed by her hurt and indignation. 'I'm not such a novice as to travel without my own funds. I'll arrange it.'

'Very well.' He seemed bored now, anxious to get things over with. And yet—there was something in his eyes, something so blank and empty that it frightened her. It was still there as he said with almost casual politeness, 'Let me know if you run into any problems.'

She nodded, speechless, as he straightened his shoulders and, after picking up his discarded jacket in one easy movement, strolled unhurriedly to the door, looked back once, and then shut it very quietly behind him.

Damaris stared after him, her nails biting hard into her palms. When, after a long time, her eyes dropped to the floor, she saw that he had left his red silk tie. She thought of knocking on his door and returning it, but dismissed the idea almost at once. It was over. And because it was over she couldn't bear to look at his face again.

'That's it,' she announced to the unresponsive air-conditioned room. 'The end of the affair that never was. And all I have left to show for it is one expensive blood-red silk tie.' Her voice cracked, and she flung herself face down on to the bed and buried her head in the pillows.

She was still lying there, too listless, too heavy in spirit to move, when the knock came at the door an hour later.

Reluctantly she rolled over and sat up. The knock came again, and without troubling to straighten her hair or the bed she dragged herself across the room to answer the summons.

Joel stood on the threshold looking very big and dark in the glow of the discreet hall lighting. He looked exhausted too, older and more careworn than she had ever seen him. But when he spoke, instead of making some momentous pronouncement all he said was, 'I'm sorry to trouble you, Damaris. I've left my tie.'

She could tell from the tone of his voice that if there was one thing on earth which didn't interest him at the moment, it was very probably his missing tie.

She jerked her head in the general direction of his property. 'Help yourself,' she said tightly.

Joel threw her one quick, enigmatic glance and walked past her as she stood leaning against the doorframe for support. He picked up the tie from the chair where she had carefully laid it, and returned to stand stiffly in front of her.

'Can I talk to you?'

Can he talk to me? He's actually *asking*, she thought bemusedly.

'I suppose so. Talk's free.' She was afraid to let herself respond with any degree of warmth. If she did, she would probably either hit him or burst into tears.

Joel nodded. 'Yes,' he agreed. 'So it is.' He paused, and then went on without visible emotion, 'I asked you to marry me, Damaris. You didn't give me an answer.'

She gasped. 'Wh-what?'

'I said you didn't give me an answer.'

'But. . . I thought. . .you don't *want* to marry me any more. Do you?'

He closed his eyes and then opened them again to stare directly and impassively into hers. 'I made you an offer,' he replied, not answering her question, 'and I don't go back on my promises.'

This time Damaris was the one who closed her eyes. My goodness, did he think that one minute he could tell her he loved her, the next say he'd changed his mind, and then come coolly back when it suited him and offer to keep a promise he'd never actually made, presumably because he'd decided it was the gentlemanly thing to do? If she'd had small pockets of doubt before, they had just turned into gaping manholes. If she accepted Joel's condescending offer now, she would be *asking* for the grief that would almost inevitably follow. How could she possibly even *think* of marrying a man so changeable and incomprehensible, so. . .so hard as Joel had shown he could be?

She clenched her fists tightly behind her back and lifted her chin, feeling stronger that way. 'Don't worry,' she said frostily. 'it wasn't really a promise and I won't hold you to it. As far as I'm concerned, a marriage between us could only end in disaster.'

'Perhaps.' He wasn't looking at her now but at a spot high up on the wall above her head. 'You said you loved me, Damaris. Was that true?'

'I'm not in the habit of lying.'

'Aren't you? I thought you were. Although mainly to yourself, I suppose.'

Damaris didn't give him the satisfaction of a fiery reaction. 'If you haven't anything civil to say, I suggest you go,' she replied coldly.

He raised his hand and rested it on the doorframe. 'If

I was uncivil, I apologise. And I expect you're right. That old saw about love making the world go round doesn't hold up too well under the day-to-day reality of a marriage that should never have happened. We both know that, don't we?'

'Yes,' said Damaris in a choked voice. 'We do.'

'Goodbye again, then. And I'm sorry if I. . .upset you.'

'You didn't upset me,' lied Damaris.

'Good.' Suddenly, to her utter amazement, he lifted his red tie and looped it around her neck, drawing her towards him, but not so close that their bodies actually touched. Then he bent his head and kissed her with such excrutiating thoroughness that she thought she would die if he carried it on much longer; either that, or throw her arms around his neck and beg him to stay.

When he had finished, he removed the tie very slowly and slung it over his shoulder. Then he stood looking down at her for a long time, the harsh planes of his face showing no signs of softening. But just before he left, to her astonishment he lifted his thumb to touch it ever so lightly to her nose.

Damaris returned to the bed where she lay, dry-eyed and sleepless, into the early hours of the morning. Then she rose quietly, showered, packed, ordered breakfast, and while most of the hotel's guests were still sleeping soundly she took a taxi to the airport to catch the first possible flight back to Vancouver.

CHAPTER NINE

'DAMSON! What the hell's happened to you? You look terrible.'

'Thanks.'

'Well, you do. Have you been ill?' Chloe glared at her friend as if being ill were a serious misdemeanour.

'In a way. And for heaven's sake stop scowling at me. Come on in and cheer me up instead.'

'You look as though you could do with some cheering,' replied Chloe, who needed no second invitation. She marched straight into the kitchen, plumped her khaki-skirted bottom into a chair and, after a closer inspection of Damaris's white and peaky face, demanded to know where she kept her brandy.

'I don't have any.'

'Well, you ought to. You look as if you could use it.'

Damaris shook her head. 'You're supposed to be cheering me up, not making rude remarks about my looks.'

'Hm. Is there any *chance* of cheering you?' asked Chloe doubtfully.

'No.'

'I didn't think so. What's the matter, Damson? The hunk again?'

'Not really. The hunk, as you call him, is no longer a part of my life.' Damaris turned her back and began to be very busy filling the kettle. 'What about you and Sebastian?' she asked in a voice that, to Chloe's ears, sounded far too bright.

158

'Sebastian is also a back-number.' Chloe grinned reminiscently. 'He wasn't bad in some ways, and Paris was wonderful, but I'm not much on astronomy and the origins of the universe at two a.m. With the history of philosophy thrown in.'

'He sounds very educational,' said Damaris, stifling the first urge to giggle she'd had in weeks.

'Oh, he was that all right. And stop trying to change the subject.'

'I'm not.'

'Yes, you are. Why are you wandering around in a housecoat this early in the evening—looking a bit like a halibut that's gone off?'

'You *are* good for my morale,' groaned Damaris, unplugging the kettle. 'First you say I look terrible, and now you're comparing me to a fish.' She sighed. 'I must be a sight to behold.'

'You are. Come off it, Damaris. Tell Auntie Chloe all about it, and after that we'll do what we can to get you back in running order.'

'Good grief, now I'm some kind of engine,' muttered Damaris.

All the same, she really was smiling now, and the urge to unburden herself into Chloe's sympathetic ear was overwhelming. She poured two mugs of instant coffee and sat down facing her friend.

'I *was* sick for a while,' she admitted, 'but that's all over with now——'

'Uh-huh. And your current sickness happens to be called Joel Agar. Am I right?'

'I'm afraid so.' Damaris stared unseeingly into her coffee, and her eyes glazed over as her mind went back over the last three awful weeks.

She had arrived back in Vancouver late at night, to

the considerable irritation of Nurse Johnston, who didn't appreciate being woken up by what she had at first assumed was an intruder. In the morning the nurse had left, mollified at receiving her full week's pay, and after that Damaris's only companions had been a disapproving Candy, who had paid her back for her desertion by ignoring her, and Ginny, who had kept asking where 'nice man' was. Which didn't help, because Damaris was missing 'nice man' quite desperately herself. The fact that she didn't think he was nice at all made no difference. She loved Joel, and she felt utterly bereft without his teasing, his kisses, his seductive smile. . .his roses. . .and, yes, even his habit of telling her what to do. She realised now that she had enjoyed their constant sparring. Without it, without *him*, her life had become empty and flat and dull. Mary and Chloe were both away, so she had been without the solace of their company as well, and her work with her girls' club and the old people could in no way assuage the desolation in her heart.

She had seen Joel's picture in the papers once, surrounded by smartly-dressed women at some civic function, and immediately she had crumpled the offending page into a ball and flung it at the empty fireplace—only to rescue it an hour later. To top off an imperfect homecoming, two days after Damaris returned Candy vanished. One moment she was there, large and malevolent-looking on the back steps, the next she had stalked off into a clump of fir trees from which she had not since emerged.

Just for a moment, when Damaris had seen Chloe's cheerful face on the doorstep, her heart had lightened; but now, sitting opposite her in the kitchen, she knew that no friend, however well-meaning, could take the place of the man she had come to love.

'Tell me,' Chloe insisted. 'It'll do you good to get it off your chest.'

Damaris returned to her surroundings with a start, smiled wanly, and in a low, broken voice, poured the whole sad story into her friend's concerned and kindly ear.

When she had finished, Chloe shook her head. 'I don't understand it,' she said. 'Why didn't you just say "yes" when he asked you to marry him, instead of regaling him with all the dreary details of your marriage?'

Damaris felt her eyes misting over. 'Because I wasn't sure. And I wanted him to understand.'

'Hm! Which he didn't.'

'No. I don't know what I said to him, but he turned all cold and contemptuous and he didn't seem to want me any more.'

'He came back though. And, like the idiot you are, you turned him down.'

'I'm not an idiot,' said Damaris, with a return of her old spark. 'You'd have turned him down too if he'd made it sound as if he was fulfilling an obligation.'

'I'd have turned him down anyway,' retorted Chloe. '*After* I'd got him into bed. You slipped up there, Damson.' She made a face. 'But then I'm not you.'

'No,' said Damaris morosely. 'You're not.'

Chloe stared down at the huge ring on her middle finger. 'Damaris, I know how unhappy you are. It shows in your eyes, in the way you look and move, in your voice. In fact you're a very depressing person to be around.' She pursed her lips thoughtfully. 'But more than likely he's unhappy too. Why don't you call him?'

Damaris shook her head. 'No.'

'Why not? Would you marry him now if he asked you?'

'How could I? He doesn't really want me any more. I don't know why, but he doesn't.'

'Mm. You could be right,' muttered Chloe. 'I suppose if he did he'd get over whatever's eating him and arrive with an armful of roses to sweeten you up.' She took a sip of coffee, then grinned suddenly, her merry eyes bright with resolution. 'Right. There's only one thing for it. We'll have to get your mind off that man.'

Damaris smiled wearily. 'Wonderful. And how do you propose to do that?'

'Simple. We'll fix you up with someone else. You might quite like Sebastian——'

'Forget it.'

Chloe looked pensive. 'Yes, on second thoughts. . . I know, how about old Clinton?'

'Thanks, but I'm not in the market for your cast-offs,' snapped Damaris, more sharply than she intended.

Chloe sighed. 'I was afraid you wouldn't be. Tell you what, I'll be generous. I'll arrange a date for you with Jeremy. He's not a cast-off.' She sighed again. 'He was going to be my next project.'

'Oh, Chloe.' Damaris didn't know whether to laugh or cry. 'Chloe, your generosity overwhelms me. It really does. But I don't *want* another man. Not ever.'

'Nonsense,' said Chloe briskly. 'Let's see now. . .'

Damaris let her ramble on.

Over the next two weeks, Chloe continued to work on Damaris, at first making endless suggestions and after a while actually parading a succession of young men through her door. Some of them were handsome, some of them artistic, some looked to Damaris like refugees from the Mafia—and some of them were even quite nice; but she treated them all with polite uninterest and tepid coffee, and in all but one case they made an excuse to leave within the hour.

The exception was Charlie McMahon. He stayed for two hours and returned for more the next day.

Charlie was an out-of-work artist who claimed to be in love with Chloe, so Damaris felt entirely safe with him. The third time he asked her to go out—to make Chloe jealous, he said—and she shrugged and accepted. She didn't think there was the remotest chance he would make Chloe jealous, but he was a pleasant enough companion and she saw no reason not to help him out. Besides, she had nothing else to do.

When Chloe heard the news, she beamed from ear to ear and insisted that Damaris put on the new topaz-coloured dress she had bought to take to New York and never worn. She also insisted on bright red lipstick and a warm blush tint for her cheeks. 'It'll put some life in your face,' she asserted. 'It's time you stopped looking like a fish.'

So much for Charlie's hopes, thought Damaris, who didn't care what she looked like. Which was probably just as well because, by the time Chloe had finished with her, she resembled a 'before and after' picture with 'before' still showing through 'after'.

Charlie looked a bit startled by her appearance, but managed to rise gallantly to the occasion.

'What a transformation,' he said, with commendably impassive restraint.

'Is it? Chloe did it,' replied Damaris who hadn't looked in the mirror. 'She said I needed brightening up.'

'Ah. I thought I detected her artistry.' He took her arm. 'Shall we go?'

The evening that followed was in marked contrast to the ones she had spent with Joel. For one thing, Charlie was out of work, and when they got to the movie they had chosen it emerged that he was also out of money. So Damaris paid for them both. After the movie, which was supposed to be a comedy but which had Damaris sniffing surreptitiously through all the love-scenes, instead of going to one of Joel's quiet and discreet night-spots they ended up at McDonald's. On the way home Charlie's car ran out of petrol. Damaris paid for that too; and to top off a less than perfect evening, the moment they drew up in front of her house, her escort, perceiving that she wasn't going to ask him in, suddenly developed half a dozen extra pairs of hands.

'What about Chloe?' cried Damaris, pushing his palm off her thigh as she searched hastily for the handle of the door.

'I've decided you're more my type, Damaris. Come on now, be a sport. . .'

She was so busy trying to evade Charlie's roaming hands that she didn't hear the car pull up behind them. He reached for her again and as she scrabbled frantically at the upholstery, still unable to locate the handle, with incredible suddenness the door beside her was wrenched open.

'Out,' said a well-known voice as she practically fell on to the pavement. 'Now.'

Most of her was already out and she needed no second urging. As she grabbed at a lamp-post to regain her balance, she heard the same voice utter a few succinct, unprintable words which left no one within earshot in any doubt that if Charlie valued his skin he'd better make himself scarce in a hurry.

The threat had the desired effect, and a moment later Damaris was facing Joel beneath the lamp-post.

'What in *hell* were you doing with that creep?' he shouted at her, so loudly that Chloe's curtain twitched.

Damaris, whose insides were tying themselves in strange, unmanageable contortions, stopped feeling stunned and breathless and began to feel angry instead. It was a familiar, almost welcome sensation.

'Charlie's not a creep,' she snapped back. 'At least. . .' she hesitated '. . . I don't think he is.'

'Then you don't think wrong. I've known that little con-artist for some time. He's been through two widows from my office in the past year. Cleaned out the first one's bank account completely. The second one was a little more canny.'

'He's not interested in me anyway,' said Damaris sulkily, feeling foolish, angry, desperate and hopeful all at the same time. 'He was only using me to pique Chloe's interest.'

'Nonsense. He specialises in widows. That was just a line, you gullible little fool.'

So now she was a gullible little fool, was she? Along with all her other faults. Well. . .perhaps she *had* been easily duped. But it didn't matter. What *did* matter was that Joel was here, shouting at her in the middle of the street and, she noted for the first time, carrying an armful of roses. What was it Chloe had said. . .? No. He was *not* going to sweeten her up. Not after the way they'd parted.

'Oh, get lost,' she said rudely. And then, not really wanting him to go, 'What are you doing here anyway?'

'At the moment, trying to control a very chauvinistic urge to teach you a lesson in courtesy you won't forget.' His fingers strummed unnervingly against his thigh.

'Huh! You're a fine one to talk about courtesy,' jeered Damaris. 'And you're not going to teach me anything, Joel Agar.'

'Mm. You're probably right. I doubt if I could anyway.'

His voice was almost without inflexion, and yet. . .*was* that a ripple of amusement she heard beneath the drily spoken words?

'Did you come for anything in particular?' she asked now, her eyes very bright in the lamplight. 'Because if you didn't——'

'Of course I did. It's almost midnight. I don't call on ladies at midnight for no reason.'

'Oh,' said Damaris, not sure if she liked the sound of that and yet terrified he would go away and leave her. Because she knew now, had known from the moment she heard his voice telling her to get out of Charlie's car, that she couldn't bear it if he left her again. 'What—what do you want then?'

'You, as a matter of fact. But not here. Let's move.'

So saying, before Damaris could frame a suitably sharp reply he had put his hand on her lower back and was propelling her up her driveway ahead of him.

'Here,' he said, reaching over her shoulder to remove her key as she rummaged ineffectually in her handbag. 'For heaven's sake, let's get this show on the road.'

'What show?' asked Damaris, as usual not sure if she wanted to kiss him or kick him.

'I'm coming to that.' He pushed the door open, and again put his hand where it had no business to shove her gently inside.

Jane Spencer's saucer eyes widened. Oh, no, thought Damaris. There goes my reputation! Mother of one leaves on date with one man, returns with another. It would be all over the neighbourhood by tomorrow. The funny thing was that somehow she didn't seem to care.

'For you,' said Joel, as soon as they were alone. He handed her the roses which had so usefully restrained his movement up until this point.

Damaris shook her head. She was obviously in love with a madman. One minute he was shouting and making threats, the next he was giving her roses. 'Thank you.' She smiled bemusedly and buried her face in the fragrant yellow blossoms. 'They're beautiful.'

'Which,' said Joel, hooking his thumbs into his belt and eyeing her disgustedly, 'is more than can be said for you this evening. What in heaven's name have you done to yourself, Damaris?'

'Done to myself?' She looked blank.

'Take a look.' He removed the roses purposefully from her arms and laid them down. Then he placed both hands on her shoulders and marched her across the room to stand in front of the big mirror that hung above the fireplace.

She saw a very white, over-made-up face in which the eyes seemed enormous and bruised because of the heavy application of mascara and green shadow. The lower half of her face was slashed with a streak of red that would have looked marvellous on a dark-skinned beauty, but only made her look like one of Dracula's more recent victims.

'Oh,' said Damaris. 'Oh, dear. Chloe.'

'I thought so.' Joel's hands dropped from her shoulders to hold her waist, and she felt the whole delicious length of him along her back. Without quite meaning to, she leaned her head against his soft black sweatshirt.

Joel looked down at her and made a face. 'Watch it. If

that warpaint comes off on my sweater, Mrs Pritchard
will be convinced that I've finally gone to the dogs.
Which will be a pity, because up until now you're the
only woman I've ever brought home whom she's been
even remotely inclined to approve of.'

Damaris frowned, unable to reconcile this gentle,
teasing Joel with the hard-faced, bitter man she had left
behind in New York. And she was afraid—terrified, in
fact, that this wonderful warmth which was stealing
through her would once again turn into ice.

'That does it,' said Joel. 'We're taking a short trip to
the bathroom to wash off that mess and that scowl, and
then you and I are going to have a long, serious talk,
Damaris Gordon.'

Her legs didn't seem to belong to her any more as,
still with his hands on her waist, he pushed her into the
blue-tiled bathroom, seized the nearest towel and began
to run warm water into the basin.

'What are you doing?' she gulped, as he moistened the
towel and started to scrub briskly at her face.

'Turning you back into a wasp.'

Damaris stood utterly still as he rubbed and patted
and stroked, and finally ran the towel roughly over her
lips. By the time he had finished, her face was all warm
and tingling—but the rest of her felt oddly numb. This
didn't make sense. What was going on? Why was she
letting him walk into her life again to take over as if he
owned her? It was as if, after her initial indignant
reaction to his cavalier dismissal of Charlie, she had lost
the ability to think, or even to move for herself. She
supposed she was afraid to think. If only she could also
lose the ability to feel!

'There,' said Joel, throwing down the towel and
studying her face with satisfaction. 'You look almost

human now. And don't you ever let that woman get near you with make-up again. She's lethal.'

'She meant well,' said Damaris faintly.

'Sure.' He ran his hand through his hair. 'I suppose I should be grateful to her in a way. I came over here earlier this evening, and she saw me and told me to try again around twelve. If I hadn't, no doubt that little creep McMahon would be here right now, trying to relieve you of your money, your body, and anything else you happened to have lying around.'

'He would *not*,' said Damaris, beginning to come back to life. 'I only went out with him because he said he was in love with Chloe.'

Joel raised his eyebrows. 'If I didn't know you better, that remark would convince me you were a thoroughly unprincipled hussy. However, in your case, I suspect it makes some sort of sense. And that's enough of this idle chatter. You and I have to talk.'

Still half in a trance, Damaris let him take her hand and tow her back into the living-room. Once there, he sat down in the nearest chair and tried to pull her on to his knee.

'The roses,' she exclaimed, darting away from him. 'I have to put them in water.'

'Hurry up.'

She didn't hurry. Everything was so dream-like that she couldn't believe it was happening, and she certainly couldn't make herself move quickly. But in the end the roses were arranged in a blue ceramic jug and she carried them back into the living-room where Joel still sat sprawled in her chair.

'Put them down,' he ordered.

Vaguely she was conscious that she ought to tell him

he had no right to order her around. On the other hand, she couldn't stand there holding the roses all night.

She put them down.

It was only then, with no defences left, with no excuse for prevaricating any longer, that she came face to face with the fact that this Joel was not the same man she had left behind in New York. His cheekbones were more pronounced now, his full, sensitive lips more finely drawn and, although he still sat and moved with the old easy arrogance, there was a hollowness about his eyes that hadn't been there before.

So. . .perhaps she wasn't the only one who had found the last weeks desolate and lonely.

'Come here, wasp,' he said softly.

Mesmerised, she obeyed him, and as soon as she was close enough he reached up to drag her on to his knees.

For a long time he sat quite still with his glossy head resting back on the chair as he gazed up at her. One hand was caressing her neck and the other curved loosely around her elbow. His eyes were pensive, brooding almost, and just when she had begun to doubt that he meant to speak at all he said very quietly, 'I'm sorry, Damaris. Do you think you can ever forgive me?'

If he went on looking at her like that, his warm amber gaze melting her veins to water, she began to think she could forgive him anything, however illegal, immoral or improbable.

She tore her eyes away and stared fixedly at a small pulse throbbing in his neck. 'I think so,' she whispered. 'What do you want me to forgive?'

'I need you to forgive me for not understanding. For being so demanding and impatient. For hurting you— because I know I have hurt you—and for being damn fool enough to let you go.'

She stopped staring at the pulse then and darted a look at his face. 'I don't think you actually did let me go,' she pointed out. 'I seem to remember that you came back and repeated your offer to marry me, and I told you I wouldn't hold you to it—that if we married it was bound to end in disaster.'

Joel's hand moved to the back of her head and tousled her soft fair hair. 'You didn't have much choice, did you? You were full of doubts in the first place, and instead of trying to relieve them I behaved like a self-centred bastard. I just assumed that, since I'd decided to marry you, naturally you'd fall in with my plans. I wanted you so much, you see, that it never occurred to me. . . Anyway, you tried to explain that you had a point of view too, and I didn't even hear what you were telling me——'

'No,' said Damaris, putting a tentative hand on his chest, 'you heard something quite different, didn't you? I still don't understand what it was.'

Joel turned his eyes to the empty fireplace. 'I'll explain in a minute. Or try to. But I want you to know, wasp. . .' he smiled wryly, as the name that had started as an accusation and somehow turned into an endearment slipped so naturally off his tongue '. . . I want you to know that I did mean it when I came back and asked you to marry me the second time. I know I put it incredibly badly, made it seem like an obligation, and of course you could only turn me down. But you see. . .' He lowered his head so that she couldn't see his eyes any more. 'You see, you'd given me one hell of a shock when you told me how you'd come to marry Scott. I was still reeling, trying to cope with that knowledge—and there you were, in the next room, planning to leave the following day. I had to do something quickly, but I was in no shape to do it right.' He grimaced. 'So I did it wrong. And I lost you. If I ever had you.' His eyes met hers again and she saw the deep shadows there—and the question.

'Oh, you had me,' she said fervently, her fingers bunching up his sweatshirt, pulling it away from his neck. 'You had me hook, line and sinker. I think you've always had me. I was just too scared—of you at first, and then of myself and of life, to take a risk, to chance being vulnerable, caring what happened to somebody who wasn't Ginny and. . .and having them care about me. It was so much easier emotionally when I had only myself to depend on. Only. . .only that's not really living, is it? Running scared for the rest of my days?'

She looked at him anxiously, waiting for an answer, willing him to understand this time.

He shook his head. 'No, it's not, but I almost made the same mistake myself. Except that when I decided I wouldn't marry again I didn't count on being terminally stung by a wasp.'

He smiled, and his smile went straight to her heart, making her so dizzy that she had to wrap her arms around his neck and cling to him for support. At once his arms encircled her and he held her very gently against his chest.

'I'm sorry, Damaris,' he said, his voice all soft and husky. 'I wanted to love you, and all I did was hurt you instead.'

The swirling in her head began to settle and she pushed herself upright to stare at him with a bewildered frown. 'Why, Joel? Why did you say my marriage to Scott shocked you? I don't understand. . .'

'No, how could you?' His arms tightened as if he was afraid she might still try to run away. But when he spoke again the timbre of his voice had hardened. For a moment it was almost as if he'd forgotten she was there.

'I fell very hard and very fast when I met Sharon,' he said slowly, his fingers curling absently over her hip. 'I told you I'd had no time for more than the most casual relationships till then. Now I had time, and I was ready. More than ready, and Sharon was young and vivacious and very pretty. She flattered my ego—unlike some wasps I could name—and I wanted her so much it actually hurt. She wanted marriage, or so she said, and I was so besotted I didn't even pause to consider that she was little more than a flighty child, while I was a mature—or supposed to be mature—man with responsibilities. We were married just over a month from the day we met.' His eyes were bleak now, veiled and very far away. 'The honeymoon was all right, of course. I don't think I saw much beyond the four corners of the bed, but as soon as life began to return to normal I realised that Sharon wasn't flattering my ego any more. In fact she seemed to find my conversation, and the fact that I actually worked, a bit of a bore. Her greatest pleasure appeared to be spending my money, and we had numerous minor battles which eventually escalated into outright warfare. Then she told me I was a middle-aged, dreary old grouch—at the ripe age of thirty, if you please—and that she'd only married me because I seemed to have an inexhaustible supply of what she wanted. . .and she wasn't referring to sex. I think I'd figured that out for myself by then anyway, and of course at that point her source of funds dried up. So she set the wheels in motion for a divorce and managed to win a very nice settlement out of me.'

'Crazy lady,' said Damaris dreamily. 'Imagine settling for money when she could have had you.'

Joel looked startled, her reaction obviously not what he'd expected. His frowning, far-away expression faded. 'I take it back about wasps not being good for my ego,' he said smugly. 'And to think I took you for another Sharon!'

'Because I married Scott, you mean?' she asked, beginning to see the light at last. She shook her head. 'And to think I thought you dumped Sharon because she bored you.'

'Did you? Well, you weren't far wrong. I assure you that by the end of our marriage she had begun to bore me quite incredibly.'

'That's different.'

'Mm. I suppose so. And now do you understand why it was such a shock to be told that the woman I wanted to marry had married another man for his money, just like Sharon?'

'Yes, I do understand, but it wasn't like that. . .'

'I know, I know. Of course it wasn't the same. For one thing, *you* were honest about it. But you see I was already in a foul temper because you wouldn't just drop into my arms like a ripe plum. And then you told me about your marriage, and—well, I know there's no excuse for me, but I reacted like a man who's had everything his own way for far too long. And, quite rightly, you told me to get lost.'

'No,' said Damaris. 'Quite wrongly.'

Joel moved his hands to her shoulders, his eyes darkening. 'Do you mean that? I came back the next morning, you know. By then I'd had all night to think things through. I knew I'd been an idiot. But you'd gone.'

Suddenly she was unbearably conscious of his lips, so close to hers, and of his strong thighs shifting deliciously under hers. She swallowed and made to stand up, but Joel's arms immediately dropped, his fingers splaying out over her hips, pinning her to him. She swallowed again and then said faintly, because she had to say something, 'Why didn't you try to see me when you came home from New York, Joel? Or had you changed your mind again by then?'

'No, I had not changed my mind,' he said roughly. 'But by then I'd had time to think some more, and I remembered you'd never said you wanted to marry me in the first place. Only that you wanted to make love to me. And at the end there you were very adamant about *not* getting married. Especially to me. So I decided I'd leave you alone until you were so crazy with wanting me that you'd come tumbling into my arms the moment I gave you the word.' He scowled ferociously. 'Instead, I found you trying to tumble out of McMahon's arms. It was a blow, let me tell you.' His eyes were gleaming at her so wickedly that she wasn't sure whether she believed he meant a word of it or not.

'Did you really think it would be that easy?' she asked him, wondering what she could do to dent his complacence and at the same time relieve the erotic cravings that were shivering up the insides of her thighs.

He grinned disarmingly, yet behind the grin she thought she could still see dark shadows. 'Heavens, no,' he groaned. 'But I hoped. Goodness knows I hoped. And I did think you needed time to work things out.'

'I see.' Damaris tried to look severe and disapproving, but only succeeded in responding helplessly to that horribly seductive grin. 'And you just happened to pick the day I was out with Charlie,' she said drily. 'Do I detect the meddlesome hand of my neighbour?'

'As a matter of fact, you don't. Something happened today and I decided I'd been without you long enough.'

'Oh, you did?' Her voice lost a little of its warmth. 'And I suppose, as usual, I have nothing to say about your—decision?'

'You have everything to say. Everything that matters. Don't start going waspy on me again, Damaris. I don't think I can take much more today.'

'All right,' said Damaris, mollified. 'What happened to make you pick today?'

To her enormous relief he removed his hand from her hips and sprawled comfortably back in the chair.

'Do you remember Mike?'

'On the *Jacqueline*? Of course.'

'His wife came back yesterday.'

'She did?' Damaris beamed. 'Oh, Joel, that's wonderful!'

He smiled. 'Mike thinks so too. He was wandering around all day looking as if he'd just been handed the moon on a silver platter. With half a dozen rainbows and several pink clouds thrown in. I wanted to hit him.'

'Joel! Why?'

'Because I was green, as well as black and purple, with envy.'

'You can't be black and purple with envy.'

'I can.'

'Joel, what are you talking about?'

'I'm talking about you, you impossible wasp. There was Mike, floating around in his own private heaven, looking like a lovesick teenager, and there was I, still in my own private hell and no doubt looking like an equally lovesick, but thoroughly disgruntled, old man. In the end Mike came out of his cloud for long enough to tell me to stop ruining his digestion and to get the hell off my own boat so he could get on with his reunion without my oppressive presence.'

Damaris choked. 'And did you?'

'Mm. I did even better. I decided that if requited love could do so much for Mike's disposition perhaps it would also work for me. If I was lucky.' He smoothed his hand through her hair, suddenly serious. 'I was going crazy without you, Damaris. I couldn't wait any longer. But, truth to tell, I've been almost afraid—I told you everyone's afraid of something—to try again. Because if you say "no" this time it will be the last time.'

Damaris looked into his eyes and saw that he meant every word. 'I see,' she said solemnly, not willing to succumb to his potent charm without a struggle. 'So you came storming over here, practically assaulted my date, washed my face without so much as a by-your-leave, and then started ordering me around. Is that the way you normally soften girls up?'

Joel's face was a study in consternation. 'Oh, no,' he groaned. 'Is that what I did?'

Damaris nodded.

'In that case my only excuse is that I *was* furious when I saw you in the clutches of that little creep. And if I hadn't shouted at you I'd very probably have taken you in my arms right then and there, made love to you in the nearest flower-bed—and blown everything.'

'Yes,' said Damaris thoughtfully. 'I've just planted marigolds in that flower-bed. I doubt if it would have done them a lot of good. And it wouldn't have been at all romantic.'

This time it was Joel's turn to choke, but after a while he sobered; then quite suddenly she found herself being tipped off his knee as he uncoiled himself from the chair and stood up, pulling her with him.

'What do you consider romantic?' he asked, to her surprise.

Damaris blinked. 'I don't know. Roses and silk and fresh clean snow. Moonlight and summer nights. . .'

Her low voice trailed off as Joel turned to lift the jug of yellow roses. 'Come on,' he said, taking her hand and towing her determinedly to the door.

'What are you doing?' she gasped as he turned the handle and, putting his arm around her waist, hustled her out into the garden.

'Roses,' he explained, waving the blue jug precariously. 'Moonlight and summer nights—night, anyway. The silk will be for your wedding dress. And if you really insist on snow I'll build you an igloo. For our honeymoon.' As Damaris gaped at him, quite suddenly he went down on one knee and, holding the roses in front of him, said with only the faint trace of a quiver in his voice, 'I love you, Charity Damaris Gordon. Maybe I'm crazy, but I do. For the third, and final time of asking—will you marry me? Because if you won't we're heading straight for that flower-bed.'

CHAPTER TEN

DAMARIS stared down at Joel, speechless for a moment as the moonlight cast dark reflections on his face. There was laughter in his voice, a gentle teasing, but when the light fell on his eyes she saw that the laughter masked uncertainty and an aching hope that matched her own desperate need.

'Yes,' she said quietly. 'I'll marry you, Joel. Of course I will.' Her voice broke. 'I didn't think you wanted me any more.'

'What?' His roar reverberated round the roof-tops as he leaped to his feet and made a lunge towards her. 'You impossible, infuriating, utterly adorable woman! How could you have thought for one moment that I didn't want you? I've been wanting you like mad since that very first time I saw you, glaring at me all white and waspy across that ballroom.' He made another lunge and a rose-thorn pierced Damaris's topaz dress.

'Do put those down,' she said unsteadily. 'I know I said roses were romantic, but I honestly didn't mean the thorns.'

'What?' He looked startled for a moment, and then gazed bemusedly at the blue jug which was still clutched firmly in his hand.

'Put them down,' repeated Damaris, laughing.

The bemused look vanished as Joel did as she suggested and stepped forward to take her into his arms.

Some seconds later, as a deep peace stole over her and

she was at last able to tear her lips from his, Damaris gasped faintly. 'Joel, wait. Ginny. She's all alone.'

'She's not alone. We're standing right under her window. And she's fast asleep.'

'All the same——'

'OK, OK,' he growled. 'So much for moonlight and roses.' Suddenly he grinned. 'Besides, if flower-beds don't take your fancy, I can think of several excellent alternatives.'

'Joel. . .?'

'But he wasn't listening. With a wolfish and very purposeful leer, he scooped her up in his arms, strode back into the house and, kicking the door shut behind him, carried her through the hall to deposit her on the soft white rug in front of the fireplace.

'It's not snow, but it's the right colour,' he said softly. 'Will it do?'

Damaris looked up at his smiling face. He was gazing at her with an expression of such tenderness, such warmth and love, that just for a moment she couldn't believe it was really meant for her, that after twenty-seven years she had at last found someone who didn't think she was a nuisance, an obligation or, at best, a convenience: someone who loved her.

She held out her arms and at once he dropped down beside her, cradling her softly yielding body against his strength.

At first Joel seemed content just to hold her, but after a while he began to trail soft kisses across her skin. When his lips reached the V of her dress he paused for a moment, lifted his head and drawled huskily, 'No barriers between us now, wasp. This has to go.'

'No barriers,' she agreed, as the blood began to curdle in her veins.

He rolled her towards him, started unfastening buttons, and as Damaris struggled to help him the dress fell away on the floor. It was followed by the flimsy wisps of fabric she wore beneath it.

Joel gazed down at her as she lay all pale and pearly in the soft light cast by the moon. His eyes were almost worshipful in the dimness. 'You're beautiful, wasp,' he murmured. 'Like a beautiful dream come true.'

'So are you,' she gasped as he pulled his sweater over his head and once more lowered himself beside her.

Very gently his hands began to feather over her thighs. His lips stroked her skin, gently too, at first, and then with deeper intensity as his tongue tasted the sweetness of her mouth.

She gave a little cry when his hand reached her stomach and then curved down to touch the most secret part of her. His kisses trailed paths of fire down the pulsing hollow of her throat and further to the swell of her breasts. Her fingers caught in his hair, spread across his hard back, and at that moment she knew that the independence she had once thought she wanted was only an illusion—because that independence had been separate, alone and lonely. The independence she had now came from being a living, vibrant half of one whole, of two people who together were more than they could ever be alone.

She closed her eyes. Thank goodness she had learned the truth in time.

'I love you, Joel,' she whispered, her lips against the flat curve of his ear.

'Damaris,' he responded, his voice like slurred velvet between her breasts. 'My lovely Damaris.'

His caresses became more demanding, drawing her into such a fever of longing that she cried out. His leg slid between her thighs as her fingers dug softly into the smooth silkiness of his back. Then they came together, and Damaris felt as if she were climbing a very steep mountain, knowing that when she reached the top everything she had ever dreamed of would be hers.

She reached the peak, sunlight glimmered in blinding flashes of silver, and as Joel's eyes blazed into hers she knew that at last she had conquered far more than a mountain. She had conquered fear, because her fear had been her own lack of love.

Joel seemed to understand as, slowly and blissfully, they drifted down from the heights, knowing they would return again and again.

'My glorious, impossible, wonderful wasp,' he murmured long afterwards as they lay in the pale light of the morning that was beginning to shimmer against the window. 'How could I ever have thought you were just some tiresome bug I needed to get out of my system?'

'Did you?' Damaris gave a tremulous giggle. 'I think I had some idea like that about you. I was so afraid for my precious security; I didn't understand that there can't be any kind of security without love.'

Joel turned his head to smile at her with lazy tenderness. 'We both had a lot to learn,' he said quietly. 'Perhaps we still have.'

'About each other? Yes, isn't it wonderful? A lifetime to spend learning about you.'

'Mm, that's very. . .' His voice trailed off. 'Damaris, have you added to your family since I left?'

'Added to my. . . No, of course not.'

'Then what are those puffballs doing parading across my sweatshirt?'

'Puffballs?' Damaris sat up abruptly, her eyes widening and her fluffy hair standing up on end. 'Joel, you don't mean. . .?'

He did.

Across the blue patterned carpet and Joel's casually discarded clothing, four diminutive Candys and one coal-black changeling trotted briskly towards the stairs; in front of them marched a much thinner Candy, head erect and bushy tail beckoning forward as if to say 'follow me'.

'Oh!' cried Damaris. 'Oh, Joel, she's back!'

'Complete with reinforcements,' he said drily. 'And you find that cause for celebration?'

She punched him absently in the stomach, making him gasp. 'Of course I do. She's been gone for weeks. And she's brought her family. Oh, Joel, they look terribly clean and looked after. Where do you suppose they've been?'

Joel sighed. 'I've no idea. The point is, they're not there any longer.'

'No,' said Damaris, reaching for her dress and beginning to struggle into it. 'They're not, are they? She was mad at me for abandoning her to Nurse Johnston, so maybe walking out was her way of paying me back.'

'I doubt it,' said Joel gloomily. 'I think she's been waiting for exactly the right time to take revenge on you. Newborn kittens aren't much trouble except to their mother. This lot, on the other hand, are starting their reign of terror on my sweatshirt.'

'What do you. . .? Oh, I see.'

The last in the parade of kittens, having decided he'd gone quite far enough, was digging his small claws busily into Joel's heaped-up clothing and appeared to be settling in for a nap. The remaining four kittens and their mother were now attempting to stumble their way up the stairs. Candy reached the top with her usual aplomb, but when she discovered that her family was still struggling behind her she went back to render assistance.

'Where are they going?' asked Joel.

'My bed, I expect.'

'Oh. You mean we're to spend tomorrow night down here as well? I can live with that.'

'I'm sure Candy's willing to share,' said Damaris innocently.

'Like hell.' Joel rolled over and sat up. 'Why are you getting dressed?'

Damaris turned her head away, still awed by his naked magnificence. 'Because I'm about to get acquainted with my new family,' she said primly, glancing at the small black bundle at her feet. 'And to take this little fellow to join his brothers and sisters.'

Joel shook his head. 'You mean you're putting your clothes on to introduce yourself to a bunch of *cats*?' he said disgustedly.

'Kittens,' she corrected. 'Of course I am. Besides, it's already morning.'

He groaned. 'Five a.m. Don't tell me you habitually rise at this ungodly hour.'

'No,' she admitted, and then added slyly, 'but I could be persuaded to, with the right incentive.'

'The only incentive you'll be getting, my girl, will be to keep your beautiful body where it damn well belongs.'

'Which is. . .?'

'In my bed.' He gave her a lazy smile, which was instantly wiped off his face as he doubled over with a howl of indignation and yelled, 'Ouch!'

'What's the matter?' asked Damaris sweetly.

'You and your bloody cats, that's what's the matter! One of them just stepped on my sensitive parts.'

'Oh, dear.' Damaris lifted her hand to hide a grin.

'It's only Candy come back for her missing kitten. But I do see that being stepped on just there could be very inconvenient,' she added quickly, when Joel seemed about to explode.

'Wasp,' he growled, reaching for her ankles and pulling her down on top of him. 'You'll find out just how inconvenient it can be if you don't watch out.'

Damaris pushed her hand through the thick brown hair on his forehead, and laughed down at him. 'I can hardly wait,' she gibed.

But as Joel's hands began to curve over her bottom she wriggled away from him and stood up. 'You'd better get dressed too,' she informed him. 'Chloe has a habit of sneaking in early to borrow eggs or something. And yes, if you were thinking of asking, she *does* have a key again. I had one made.'

'Damn,' said Joel. 'I can see it's high time you moved to my place.' But he took her advice and began to pull on his jeans.

'Mm,' agreed Damaris. 'I suppose we don't need two houses, do we? And I like yours best.'

'Just as well. You'll need Mrs Pritchard to help you with all those kids you'll be raising. Not to mention kittens,' he added glumly.

'No more kittens,' she promised, peering at him doubtfully. 'What do you mean, all those kids? I thought you didn't want any.'

'He paused in the act of fastening his belt, his eyes no longer laughing. 'You mean you'd give up the chance to have more kids if I asked you?'

Damaris stared at the cat-hairs clinging to his sweat-shirt. 'I've got Ginny,' she replied in a small voice.

'And she's enough?'

'Not really. I want to have your child, Joel. But if you don't——'

Her words were cut off abruptly as Joel's arms swept around her and she was lifted completely off her feet. 'Oh, my darling wasp!' he exclaimed. 'Thank you for your willingness to make that sacrifice. But of course I want your children. Not a football team, please. Maybe a nice conservative two—just so Mrs Pritchard doesn't walk out on us. She's been on about a family for years. And a suitable wife, of course; for some reason she's decided you'd fall into that category rather well.' He grinned. 'I can't think why.'

The only bit of him she could conveniently get her hands on was his hair, so she gave it a good, sharp tug, and he let out a shout of laughter and put her down.

'Watch it, or I'll shave it all off,' he threatened, giving her bottom a gentle pat.

Damaris was still trying to think of a satisfactorily crushing reply when her train of thought was interrupted by a demanding shriek from upstairs.

'Mama. Mama. Nice man. Nice man back.'

'You should take a leaf from your daughter's book,' said Joel smugly. '*She* has a most commendable appreciation for my good points.'

'So have I,' grinned Damaris, her hand creeping towards his belt buckle.

'Wasp,' he muttered, catching it and holding it behind her back. Then he bent his head and kissed her very soundly, before releasing her to collect his excited junior fan-club from upstairs.

'Bother,' said Damaris three days later when the phone rang shrilly as she and Joel sat peacefully in the garden enjoying the evening sun, and making plans for a quiet wedding to be attended only by family and close friends.

Reluctantly she went into the house to answer the insistent summons.

She was gone for some minutes, and by the time she came back Joel was glancing impatiently at his watch.

'Anything important?' he asked.

'You might say so,' said Damaris vaguely, trying to conceal a smile and not succeeding.

'Might I?'

'Mm. That was Mary. She's back.'

'Ah, the traveller has returned, has she? Now tell me why I should think that's important.'

'Well, she did bring us together. But I hadn't had a chance to tell her that her machinations have finally paid off. She's come up with this wonderful new scheme, Joel.'

'Oh?' he replied suspiciously. 'And what's that?'

'Well, apparently their last mystery date banquet was such a success that they've decided to hold another. But for men this time. With a woman as the masked mystery.'

Joel grinned. 'And did she tell you who they're trying to con into it this time?'

'Yes,' said Damaris, gazing pensively up at the clouds. 'It seems they're having trouble getting anyone with a high profile. So they've given up and decided to ask me.'

Joel's roar raised more than the roof-tops this time: it raised Candy and five kittens, Ginny and Jane Spencer, who were just coming in from a walk, and Chloe and Mary, whose heads appeared over their fences at the same moment.

Joel took one look at his audience, grabbed Damaris by the hand and shouted, 'Now that I have your attention, hear this all of you. I'm going to marry this woman. And the only mystery date she's going on is with me. Anyone opposed?'

Nobody was.

'Good,' he said loudly, raising a protesting trio of birds from a plum tree. 'In that case the matter is hereby closed. Permanently. And so is your mouth, my sweet,' he added in a normal voice, as he turned quickly and caught Damaris laughing up at him.

He was right, as it happened, but only because he closed it with a kiss.

HARLEQUIN®

my Valentine
1993

The most romantic day of the year is here! Escape into the exquisite world of love with MY VALENTINE 1993. What better way to celebrate Valentine's Day than with this very romantic, sensuous collection of four original short stories, written by some of Harlequin's most popular authors.

**ANNE STUART
JUDITH ARNOLD
ANNE McALLISTER
LINDA RANDALL WISDOM**

THIS VALENTINE'S DAY, DISCOVER ROMANCE WITH MY VALENTINE 1993

Available in February wherever Harlequin Books are sold. VAL93

COME FOR A VISIT—TEXAS-STYLE!

Where do you find hot Texas nights, smooth Texas charm and dangerously sexy cowboys? CRYSTAL CREEK!

This March, join us for a year in Crystal Creek...where power and influence live in the land, and in the hands of one family determined to nourish old Texas fortunes and to forge new Texas futures.

CRYSTAL CREEK reverberates with the exciting rhythm of Texas. Each story features the rugged individuals who live and love in the Lone Star State. And each one ends with the same invitation...

Y'ALL COME BACK...REAL SOON!

Watch for this exciting saga of a unique Texas family in March, wherever Harlequin Books are sold.

CC-G

HARLEQUIN®

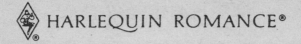

HARLEQUIN ROMANCE®

Norah Bloomfield's father is recovering from his heart attack,
and her sisters are getting married. So Norah's feeling a bit
unneeded these days, a bit left out....

Orchard Valley

And then a cantankerous "cowboy" called Rowdy Cassidy
crashes into her life!

"The Orchard Valley trilogy features three delightful, spirited
sisters and a trio of equally fascinating men. The stories are rich
with the romance, warmth of heart and humor readers expect,
and invariably receive, from Debbie Macomber."
—Linda Lael Miller

Don't miss the Orchard Valley trilogy by Debbie Macomber:

VALERIE   Harlequin Romance #3232 (November 1992)
STEPHANIE   Harlequin Romance #3239 (December 1992)
NORAH   Harlequin Romance #3244 (January 1993)

Look for the special cover flash on each book!

Available wherever Harlequin books are sold.

HARLEQUIN®

THE TAGGARTS OF TEXAS!

Harlequin's Ruth Jean Dale brings you
THE TAGGARTS OF TEXAS!

Those Taggart men—strong, sexy and hard to resist...

You've met Jesse James Taggart in FIREWORKS!
Harlequin Romance #3205 (July 1992)

And Trey Smith—he's THE RED-BLOODED YANKEE!
Harlequin Temptation #413 (October 1992)

Now meet Daniel Boone Taggart in SHOWDOWN!
Harlequin Romance #3242 (January 1993)

And finally the Taggarts who started it all—in LEGEND!
Harlequin Historical #168 (April 1993)

Read all the Taggart romances!
Meet all the Taggart men!

Available wherever Harlequin Books are sold.

ROMANCE IS A YEARLONG EVENT!

Celebrate the most romantic day of the year with MY VALENTINE! (February)

CRYSTAL CREEK
When you come for a visit Texas-style, you won't want to leave! (March)

Celebrate the joy, excitement and adjustment that comes with being JUST MARRIED! (April)

Go back in time and discover the West as it was meant to be . . . UNTAMED—Maverick Hearts! (July)

LINGERING SHADOWS
New York Times bestselling author Penny Jordan brings you her latest blockbuster. Don't miss it! (August)

BACK BY POPULAR DEMAND!!!
Calloway Corners, involving stories of four sisters coping with family, business and romance! (September)

FRIENDS, FAMILIES, LOVERS
Join us for these heartwarming love stories that evoke memories of family and friends. (October)

Capture the magic and romance of Christmas past with HARLEQUIN HISTORICAL CHRISTMAS STORIES! (November)

WATCH
DETAILS
HARLE